Hafid Bouazza was born in Oujda, Morocco in 1970. He moved to the Netherlands at a young age, studied Arabic and worked as a teacher and translator of Arabic. *Abdullah's Feet* is his first book. He has recently published a novel, *Momo*, to wide acclaim.

Ina Rilke is the translator of Margriet de Moor and Cees Nooteboom. She was awarded the 1999 Vondel Prize for Translation.

ABDULLAH'S FEET

Hafid Bouazza

Translated from the Dutch by Ina Rilke

review

Translation © 2000 Ina Rilke

First published in 2000
by REVIEW

An imprint of Headline Book Publishing

10 9 8 7 6 5 4 3 2 1

ISBN 0 7472 7309 X

Printed and bound in Great Britain by
Clays Ltd, St Ives plc.

Typeset by
Letterpart Limited
16 Bell Street, Reigate, Surrey

Headline Book Publishing
A division of the Hodder Headline Group
338 Euston Road
London NW1 3BH
www.reviewbooks.co.uk
www.hodderheadline.com

Contents

Ghost Town	7
Abdullah's Feet	19
Love Under the Olive Tree	33
Satanic Eggs	45
Lord of the Flies	69
Apolline	95
Prodigal Son	105
The Fisherman and the Sea	117

Ghost Town

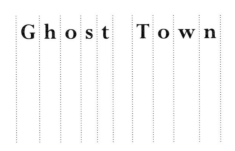

'Sibawayh!'

The silence shifted uneasily like a bashful woman in male company.

I called again. It was always the same ritual, ever since the day he had exchanged his place on my cot for the stable down below. Perfidious Sibawayh. My impatience, his maddening sluggishness.

'Sibawayh!'

This time I tap-tap-tapped with my tremulous walking stick (silver-knobbed) hard on the floor.

Silence.

Some commotion, a cough, the a-metrical creak on the stairs and suddenly my gloom was filled with evil-smelling, swishing Sibawayh: he was undoubtedly adjusting his hurried clothing. Brusquely he helped me into my cloak.

'What a stench . . . what a stench . . .' I muttered, leaning on his low shoulder. He slipped 'those-yes-yes-those' babouches on to my feet and smoothed the hood of my cloak. 'Now go and saddle the mule,' I told him.

There was a time when mule and harness were matters of grave concern to me. Like all men of rank I had a predilection for the female animal, preferably dappled, sleek, nib-eared, the mane and tail plaited, the croup drum-sized. As for the harness, the caparison had to be brocaded, or at least veined with the illusion of gold thread. Scrofulous beggars with watery eyes, hands ever cupped, would gape at the silk and gold of bridle and stirrup as at the splendours of after-worldly promise. Both legs had to rest over the left flank, swinging gently from the knee, the cloak arranged in even folds, the feet shod in velvet-covered slippers. It was quite an art to affect boredom while holding the reins between thumb and curved little finger, and not only to conduct one's mount with delicacy but also (when accompanied by two servants) to keep the eyes fixed ahead, over the pitching gait of the slave holding the bridle, and never to allow idle thoughts of vanity to draw one's gaze to the black sun-soaked parasol-bearer at one's side.

But now it was night and for various reasons I only visited my physician after sundown. Sibawayh returned to the stable. I stood in the room and waited, a quaky old man. Memories are unpredictable, except at moments of pitiful helplessness. A blind elder, a couple of centuries old, with shrunken untoothed jaws, is invariably both helpless and to be pitied.

Sibawayh's youthful sullenness had, as was entirely to be expected, worsened over the years. Yet life (and here the wheels of memory turned again) had so indulged this once hollow-backed, round-bellied, blinking, half-naked slip of a boy. From the far end of a cramped blundering darkness (Sibawayh swore as he stumbled down the stairs) a slanting sunbeam of memory flared in my mind's eye: a prismatic burst of blinding sunshine and blazing colours, meandering multitudes, tumult, a grimace of sunny cruelty. The slave market: bare heads baking in the sun, vivid turbans and canopies, corrupt shadows. Beyond the slave market stood the great azure mosque, its back unaccountably turned to us. Slaves, both male and female, stood on display in a long gallery, running the gamut of pale and luminous to gleaming black; warm nipples, cool bellies. And there he stood, dazed, eyebrows knitted against the glare, a hint of orphan's sorrow around the corners of the mouth, arms folded behind the back (weathered elbows), jutting shoulder blades: there stood Sibawayh, nakedly exposed, obedient to the hands of the deafening broker invoking the sun's help in his exposition of the state of the four-foot-high young Sibawayh's health: the imperfect teeth, the endearing little pouch, the promise (unkept) of muscular development in his tender arms.

Mule-high, I gazed out over the multitude, my parasol-bearer at my side. I fell, forgive me, very nearly to the ground. Suddenly my precious dazzling white robes struck me as hopelessly cheap and unsuitable. By some miracle I managed to conclude the transaction without unseemly haste. Overcome with emotion I yanked the reins and left the market. A servant followed behind with Sibawayh.

And since that day, the day when (moneybag on my right hip lightened, loins weighted with ample promise of ecstasy) I first led him, Sibawayh, to my dwelling, where I bathed him (his sun-brined skin warm as sand) and then took him, naked except for a fine mousseline wrap, smelling of apple orchards, to my cool room — since that day he had been nothing but intractable, runty, all elbows. His body grew more slowly than the sores on my skin. Amid draperies patterned with hunting scenes, spent after my exertions for a shameful Venus, the stout goat of my loins lolled on my belly, soiled, reeking of Sibawayh's puckered profundity. Propped up on his bleached elbows he lay silently weeping, the nape of his neck furrowed and a trough between his jutting shoulder blades. The cleft of his hillock was smeared with blood — and the goat resumed his grazing.

My spacious and tastefully appointed suite, from the steamy kitchens to the awninged gate, put him in good cheer. Daubs of light and shade had free play with him when he ran about in the courtyard during the siesta (the only time he was permitted to leave my side).

Only rarely did he slide an anxious, inquisitive glance into the gold-dusted stable. He never wore the pretty pampooties I had given him, and would weep when forced to put them on. No doubt he still felt the stony plains of his fatherland under the soles of his feet.

In my blind state this period of my life is a playground of sunny reminiscences, a pool of light in my greedy memory. In my private darkness Sibawayh eluded me, like a mouse too swift to be seen. He existed only in so far as he breathed, moved about or spoke, which he did less and less in my presence and more and more (in that same order), alas, in the stable, that nether world where he made his belated rediscovery of youth.

I heard him curse the mule. I heard him shuffle about. I heard a door open and then shut. I heard a heavy key drop on the flagstone with a clear high clink. I heard his step-step-step on the stairs.

I held out my hand for him to guide me and leaned on him as we proceeded through the corridor and down the naked stairway, past empty rooms, along the gallery, across the roofless courtyard, past the defunct fountain into the vestibule and then down the steps to the main gate: a cautious progress through a languishing house, as smooth and perfect as a womb.

At the gate I heard the jingle-bells on the old mule's bridle. He guided my feet into the stirrups and hoisted me effortlessly on to the saddle, whereupon I shifted from one buttock to the other with a lamentable lack of grace, while keeping both legs over the left flank: a shrivelled fruitlet of life.

The house of our renowned Jewish physician was a few streets eastward, beyond the great mosque. He had subjected me to various treatments, all to no avail; salves and ointments redolent of summery lavender – a physician's cunning sense of poetry. And all the while my skin continued to break out in suppurating sores while Sibawayh felt smoother than ever to my infrequent touch. I knew what he was doing on the pallet in the stable, I knew how he lured ungodly maidens and beggars' daughters to celebrate his long-dormant lust. Each thrust wounded me. Indifferent to my heartache, he kept thrusting to the hilt.

My days of noble pursuits are over, my pride is awash in threadbare purple, the fool has vanquished the king, my writing quivers, I live in a portable darkness, my bowel movements give cause for concern. My prose resembles the spectres of my memory: empty vessels, truncated epithets drifting soulless in a ghost town where even my language is dead.

'To the physician,' I said.

He took hold of the reins and we set off at a slow pace. The mule shook its head and evaporated in a thousand tinkles. I turned back the edge of my hood. I laid my right hand open-palmed on my lap and crossed the heel of one foot over the instep of the other.

An inexplicable repugnance stirred in me. Suddenly the road dipped and my stomach lurched. This must be the alley frequented in the daytime by beggars trailed by ragged broods, their souls bared in a bowl or cupped palm. Some of them – legless, sightless, or in some other way disorderly – spent the night huddled in doorways and nooks. Some, too, persisted sleepless in their labour.

We would soon pass the door that had been painted a livid green to signal the resident's pilgrim status, to summon the mumbled blessings of beggars. The pilgrim himself had recently died a dishonourable death, leaving his reprobate sons to care for their aged mother, who had previously lost her first husband, likewise a pilgrim, and who would survive her two sons as well.

The night was a veritable poem of sounds, from Sibawayh's footfall to my hoofs: a lullaby to the pounding in my old temples. To my right sounded the far-off clamour of a demon's wake – travesties of the sense of hearing. There was a cave on the mountain of Tawbad, which backed the town, where a spring slumbered and monsters and prophets were born.

'A pittance, lord!'

The road had suddenly acquired a voice and hands, and began to tug at my cloak.

'Alms,' the hand begged, 'a pittance for a man in need!'

I am repelled by beggars, particularly beggars whose rags belie their rhetorical skills. Here was a true poet of the wayside, a master if you will of mendicant eloquence who, glutted with inspiration, awaited with hungrily bated breath the passing of audible riches. He was also desperate, and hung on to my precious slippers for dear life. The scuffle did not last long. Sibawayh came to my rescue and the miscreant made off with my babouches. Both of us barefoot now, we proceeded on our way.

The streets narrowed and I sensed that we had entered the Jewish quarter. Ivied archways sent down fluttery tendrils like rabbis' beards. A salvo of sensory stimuli: a cascade of flying vermin, the rank smell of the dungheap, a sudden braying, feathery whirrings, squawking, barking and howling. Hurried footsteps – an interrupted dalliance?

We were nearing the end of the street. As I trailed my fingers along the walls, doors sank warily into the secure embrace of their ancient arms, which soon reopened to form a modest square. Our shadows flitted to the other side.

We entered a gently sloping street. Other cobbles, other sounds. A final turning and we found ourselves in the main square, where the slave market was held by day in the cheer of the noontide sun. Beyond rose the mosque, from which a side-alley to the north-east led to the hell of tanneries and abattoirs. Running off the square in a north-westerly direction was a backstreet where those in the know could locate a small brothel, low-entranced and lavishly creepered. A rain butt by the door stood on guard, lidless and wrinkly.

Each time I touched the water in the butt before going in it would break out in a smile, believing my fingertips augured a shower. The old men in the mosque went through the same motions, with a different cistern.

This was the brothel to which I had paid many a hooded visit in the course of a nonchalant, manicured stroll – always with young Sibawayh in attendance. At the other end of the courtyard, guarding the much-frequented latrine, stood another rain butt, and yet another in the corner. They seemed to have taken the place of watchdogs. Even the host (corpulent, immaculate, a rosary in his fastidious hands) had the size and girth of a rain butt.

In my memory images of this brothel glide by in a wheeling masquerade: the swish of clothing, gleaming buttocks, well-turned calves. My moist nose, my dry throat. A smeared crack. My rhythmic spasms in the swaying dark, the room draped with tapestries depicting a young doe eyeing the hunter across her shoulder, the hunter standing scissor-legged, with a relaxed proprietary air while aiming his spear, and then Sibawayh's face crumpling up in a grimace of searing pain.

Why did I always think it was raining when I was secluded in those dimly lit rooms? I even fancied I could hear the patter of raindrops – only to step outside under gold and azure.

One day I took Sibawayh to a garden at some distance from the town. On a little stream in the sun-glanced shade he watched a duck with a downy flotilla in her wake, and she had splashed and plopped so madly that he had been afraid the poor thing was drowning. I can still see his eyes, in which the tears and the dragonflies and the sun had cut diamonds.

Further off, outside the garden, in the hellish glare, a shepherd and his flock slept away the bleached, baking noon.

Was midnight upon us already? We went past the mosque and after a while we approached the physician's tall house. Behind it loomed the awesome mountain of Tawbad. It was on that mountain that a leprous fool, a self-professed prophet, had sought refuge from the world – no prophet without a mountain. The hostile populace had pelted him with stones, which had moved him to put a curse on the town before he fled, broken and bleeding profusely. His sole companion was a donkey. He had not returned since – a farcical ascension to heaven.

We halted in front of the physician's door. My repugnance was undiminished. A sense of tedium came over me. There was nothing left to be distracted by – my memory had come to rest, it was spent. What did it matter? What of my affliction and what of Sibawayh – above all Sibawayh? What was there to stop me from grinding everything underfoot and having done with it? When all is said and done the end is only a question of dignity.

And at that moment, out of nowhere, a stick, glowing with malignant ardour, struck my brittle spine, and while the pain still throbbed in my head there came a second blow, this time to my shoulder. I had hardly the time to savour the ecstatic stiffening that pain can induce, for the blows came hard and fast, methodically aimed now at my left side and then my right. It all happened so quickly, there was no distinguishing between the pain in each limb. After a blow to my neck, the expert beating proceeded crownwards. Eventually I surrendered to the unrelenting thwack-thwacking. For a split second of weightlessness (tumbling backwards off my saddle) the safety of the ground seemed dizzyingly far away. A leaden ball turned in my gut as I cowered on the ground trying to call out for Sibawayh, but my stiff tongue could not dislodge the words from the gush of vomit.

Abdullah's Feet

My father, having kissed the pages, shut the Koran with a good-natured clap which flurried the light.

There sits my father: on a shaky wooden divan in the zebra light of the barred sun on the thatch roof, a red Koran in his hands, white-turbaned, white-bearded, a bookish frown on his forehead, scrawny, shrunken, wizened, as if he were made of the same wood as the stick by his side: a Pinocchio in the dusty workshop of my memory. My father signals the end of his reading with a pious sigh. Shades of traditional shame haunt me, intent on preventing me writing an autobiographical story.

On Friday 22 October 1977, my father shut the Koran with a sigh, but his lips kept up their mumbled rumination. In the dark chasm dividing me from the landscape of my past I still hear that murmur: outlines of words, a slurping of hot-baked divinity, the flash of a gold tooth. Then a few stones roll down into the depths, disturbing my Arcadia.

My father shut the Koran in the light of that Friday sun. It was time to make ready for prayer. A female hullabaloo reached his ears from the kitchen. Giving a groan of geriatric inertia, he wondered what could be the matter. It was clear that someone – a woman, his wife: my mother – was wailing.

'Fatima!' he called out to my mother – his wife. 'Fatima! Wife of misfortune, come here! What is going on?'

A Fatima – not my mother but my eldest sister – came running. We had all learned to obey his wishes without delay. Hesitation was fatal. Fatima's eyes were swollen from crying, but he did not notice, for he was not in the habit of looking into the eyes of his daughters once they had reached a certain age.

'What is it, Baba?' Fatima asked.

'What is all the commotion?' My father, Sheik Abdullah, jutted his chin toward the kitchen.

'It's Mother,' replied Fatima, 'she dreamed of Abdullah last night.'

Abdullah was my eldest brother and Father had forbidden us to speak of him since the day he (Abdullah, my eldest brother) had joined the army to fight a Holy War. He had appeared in my mother's dreams quite often of late, but she had obeyed my father's command and said nothing. Now her vow of silence had apparently succumbed to these insistent dreams.

'Bring your mother here,' he said. He was clearly annoyed by her mention of Abdullah.

Fatima, my eldest sister, went away and Fatima, my mother, came into the room.

'What is it, Baba?' she asked.

It is not merely for the sake of literary convention that I would like to describe my mother at this point, but also to satisfy my own curiosity and no doubt that of my readers too. But remembrance is biased, my own memory prudish, my rear-view mirror clouded. Nowadays, I remember my mother almost solely in terms of her clothing, her aroma and her reproach. The latter two are so tightly bound up with my heart as to preclude public exposure – the former can do no harm.

Here stands Fatima, my mother, face to face with me and the reader. In spite of the cascade of clothing her figure is clearly defined. The splayed pleats intimate a comforting plumpness. To be honest, not an exceptional woman: stout, shaped by the exigencies of Arab maternity. The wealth of bosom and loins suggests a diva: the prodigious posterior harks back – rather literally – to black Africa. These distinctive charms are traditionally loved by Arabs: ostrich-down cushions for the spasmodic euphoria of manly release (forgive me, Father).

My mother said she had dreamed that one of her molars had fallen out with a lot of blood, which was the cause of her hand-slapping lamentations: she was convinced that her son, my brother, Abdullah, had been killed in battle. Her body was still quaking with violent grief as she said this, but my father growled to show his disapproval of such womanly superstition.

And growl is the word. My father was never well-spoken: in fact, I sometimes wonder if he could be said to speak at all. He growled, he muttered – his chief occupation, really – he grunted and availed himself of other like sounds. Sometimes, I think, his mouth did not actually move, as if the sound came out of his nostrils or even his ears. Since his vocal cords did not get much exercise, it is strange to recall his constant throat-clearings and expectorations of greenish phlegm. His ever-furrowed brow (not high, for he lowered) wore a severe frown, as if to barricade his thoughts. But perhaps his features were nothing but the lines of a safety-deposit box, storing the documents necessary for admission to Paradise. In any case: a gratifying character.

And in any case my mother was to cease her jeremiads and disregard her dreams. She helped him to his feet and into his slippers. He would go to the mosque and pray for Abdullah. He would wash now and she could return to the kitchen.

Reassured, my mother withdrew to the kitchen, that dark corner where I spent so much of my childhood. Now I am back there again, running around in the steamy fragrance of food and fresh bread and groping my sister Fatima when she bends over. Indeed that is how I remember my sisters and mother: mostly as the curves of a stooping body. I see my sisters and mother blurring together, bending, bending, bending over to wash my morning face, to take the bread out of the clay oven, to retrieve a fallen bangle from the suds, to help a swooning sister to her feet, to . . . whatever.

Eventually I was chased out of the kitchen with a smack on the back of the head, my hand still hot with carnal discovery, and I made for the latrine before it could be occupied by my father. A father in the privy before Friday prayer is the scourge of a child's impatient bladder. But in the rush and excitement I forgot to lock the door of my private donor-bank and not long after, just as a world of vertical smiles (my bending sisters) was about to be flushed away in a vertiginous daze, a blow to my still twitching buttocks sent me packing. My father was outraged. He called me a dog and a devil and a son of sin and then shook his head almost sadly. His disgust was aroused not so much by my seedless spillage as by the fact that, despite all his warnings, I was still using my right hand instead of my left. As with most childhood experiences, the implications of his advice were lost on me *then*; *now* I am far more appreciative of the merits of ambidexterity in the wonderland of single-handed relief.

Still shaking his head my father Sheik Abdullah locked himself into the small privy and hunkered down for a cross piss and *sforzando* stool. Then he enjoyed arpeggios of water during a paperless, left-handed, ballock-bouncing ablution. And after a thorough cleansing, Father left the privy, divinely purified and dripping pizzicato.

Fatima and Fatima helped Sheik Abdullah into his cleanest jellaba and sprinkled him with the same perfume (imported from Saudi Arabia) that the prophet himself is supposed to have used. When he was ready, immaculately white and prophetically scented, he leaned on his stick while my mother and sister kissed his hand. Without a goodbye he made his way outside in a vision of chiaroscuro (thanks to the thatch roof). Goats chewed and chickens clucked around the door. He brushed aside the bleating goats — while the chickens scattered like kitchen maids in an old farce — and stepped into the street. Friday greeted him festively with garlands of light and the belligerent cries of children playing marbles, whom I had joined, my buttocks still smarting. We were so engrossed in our game (which would soon lapse into a fight) that we did not notice Father and did not interrupt our play to greet him respectfully, as was the custom. Even the female onlookers, my little sisters, were so transfixed in the hollow-backed stance of non-participation that they did not see Father.

In those days we children were not yet taken to the mosque. My father regarded a child in a mosque as a flatulent monstrosity, rather than a token of lifelong piety. So my relationship with mosques did not develop until later, and not in the country of my birth. I do not know the dizzying profusion of architectural Islam; I know only improvised places of worship with a Jerusalem of musk, incense and socks.

On his way to the mosque my father Abdullah came upon his son-in-law Abdullah — my brother-in-law — husband of my newly-wed and pregnant sister Fatima. Abdullah kissed his father-in-law's hand — the same hand my father then raised to his mouth by way of reciprocated greeting. During his wife's pregnancy (a time during which a man is not permitted to lie with his wife) my brother-in-law Abdullah had become an ardent disciple of the Maliki school, which offers a welcome alternative for the needs of men in times of frontal abstinence. I seem to remember having eavesdropped on an amorous manoeuvre between him and my pregnant sister in their room, after which he muttered: 'May God give our good mullahs — our saviours in times of hardship — a thousand blessings.'

He and my father made their way mosquewards in silence. Both shared the deep-seated, pristine alleviation which comes after voiding the bowels. And that same tingle which arises from interior and exterior cleansing, that bulwark of hygienic immunity — that is, I think, the essence of Islam. The soul resides in the gut. This has left me with a sexual obsession for women performing certain sanitary acts.

To make up for my defeat at marbles and the ensuing fist-fight, I shut myself away again and castigated my painful hand. The universe shook and buckled on quaking knees, exploded – and balance was restored. Gravity dragged at my calves like a beggar clawing the hem of a passer-by. Semi-satisfied I went back to the kitchen, where my mother would find other causes for delight.

The muezzin's nasal countertenor blaring through megaphones called the faithful to prayer. The mosque had opened its jaws wide to swallow a great stream of patient believers: the hubbub inside, which I can hear at this very moment, must be the machinery of its digestive tract.

I lose sight of my father and brother-in-law in the melee: the multitude clots and melts and I can only just catch a glimpse of the preparations inside – angels shedding their wings, the splash of water – before the crowd is engulfed in the cool gloom, and the eye of memory shuts contentedly.

Meanwhile my mother would find other causes for delight.

I had returned to the kitchen, feeling empty and listless. Digging my hands into my trouser pockets, I idled back and forth between the kitchen and the well in the courtyard, listening to my obscene words reverberating in the pit, falling down, down, down like Joseph.

I tried to catch a fly with my hands, studied a beetle that seemed to have lost its way, held my foot over that same beetle and brought it down slowly and accurately. I watched my sister and mother busying themselves about the kitchen. My sister tried to chase me away once more, but I dodged her with a bored shrug.

Now and then my mother, without interrupting her work, would burst into loud sobs, thinking of her son Abdullah, and my sister would console her, whereupon she would compose herself for a moment. She paid no attention to me, although she always warned me not to hang around in the kitchen among the women or I would never grow a beard when I was a man. And normally she would have made me take a siesta. Even my snot-smeared sleeves and fly-ridden face failed to draw her attention that afternoon.

Suddenly there was a knock on the door. My sister went to open it, as my mother did not have my father's permission to answer an anonymous knock. A moment later we heard my sister fall to the ground with a harrowing scream. My mother wiped her hands on her apron and rushed to the door, followed by my curiosity.

'Mother! Mother!' The cries issued from an emotional, empty doorway.

Mother looked left and right, but there was no one to be seen. The empty street (where have my brothers and sisters got to?) stared at us blankly.

'Mother! Mother! It's me!' the emptiness cried out.

Mother thought it wise to gather up my sister's body lying at her feet, so as to get a better view.

Then she saw.

'Mother! Mother! It's me, Abdullah, your son! Your son has come home!'

On the ground, in front of the doorstep, stood Abdullah: two feet, cleanly amputated above the ankles and topped by what looked like slices of salami. The ankles were dusty and the toenails black from the long march. The imprint of sandals, no doubt worn out on the way and discarded, was visible. The veins were swollen. Unmistakable: it was my brother, Abdullah.

Mother did not faint. Mother was, and is, a sturdy woman. At this extremity of my life I can still hear how, in the doorway to that same life, Mother burst out in awesome jujubilation. The entire street, if not the entire village – in any case my whole room right now – began – begins – to shake.

Amid cries of 'My son! My son!' my mother embraced Abdullah's feet and pressed them to her ample bosom. Her cheeks were wet with tears.

'My son! My son! My son has returned!' A crowd of neighbourhood women and children gathered inquisitively around Mother's transports of delight. Abdullah's feet were borne aloft like a trophy, and the exuberance of the swelling throng bordered on hysteria as more people came running.

Like a Bride's Train we Children followed the Multitude of Women headed by my Mother bearing

Abdullah to the Mosque: I know of no better way to express the intoxicating glory of that moment than the Teutonic use of capital letters. Abdullah's return, or rather the return of what was left of him, meant more than a personal victory: it also meant the triumph of the Holy War, which was why our instinct directed us to the mosque.

The procession went all the way around the village before arriving at the mosque at last. Prayer had not started yet, as the imam was still delivering his sermon which, reasonably enough, dealt for the most part with the Holy War and the burgeoning ranks of martyrs in Paradise. A look of amazement crossed the imam's face – amazement at the avalanche of bareheaded women spilling into the mosque – then he frowned and opened his mouth in outrage. But when my father Abdullah set eyes on my brother Abdullah held aloft in my mother's hands he praised God in an astonishingly loud voice, whereupon the imam's expression cleared and he banged his long stick on the minbar to silence the congregation.

'Let us,' he spoke in a halting voice, 'pray to God and thank him for this blessed day. And,' he added, 'let the women cover their heads at once.'

I never saw my parents in better spirits than in the days that followed.

Our small dwelling, which always seemed to sag under my father's heavy frown, heaved a sigh of relief at his beaming forehead. He sat on his wooden divan with Abdullah's feet beside him from morning until night, and together they read aloud from the Koran. Now and then we could hear snatches of Abdullah's accounts of bloodshed and triumph during the Holy War and how the Enemy was defeated. ('Praise be to God,' muttered my father, 'Praise be to God.') From time to time they received visitors, among whom the imam was a most welcome guest. In the kitchen my mother worked harder than ever. We children were kept well away from Abdullah; we were made to eat in the kitchen, as the living room was reserved for my father and him. They were served the best food on the best china (the china service, my mother's pride, kept especially for visitors); she had regard for Abdullah's feet alone. We were not so much neglected as left to our own devices. I had free play with my vulnerable and budding sisters: my mother was deaf to their dutiful protestations anyway. I hid out in the privy with the not entirely unwilling girls, and whiled away the tedious siesta by the well.

But jealousy struck eventually and one day Abdullah's feet were suddenly gone.

My mother's hysteria was beyond description. Abdullah was nowhere to be found. We children stood around her, guiltily silent, while she poured blame upon herself.

My father had different ways of expressing his sorrow. He had his holy book in which to find suitable models of paternal grief in other, far holier fathers. He reclines on his wooden divan once more.

He has aged in the space of a few pages, seems close to death, buried in a light that seems so much duller now. His lips move as he reads the chapter on Joseph in the Koran.

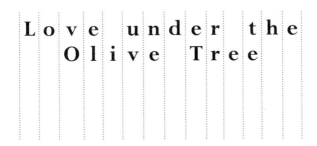

Love under the Olive Tree

A month later evening found us on the crest of a hill: three figures sharply defined against an unclouded sunset. With fingers sticky from picking olives we totted up our earnings. Thirty dirham. Each would have thirty dirham. Thirty dirham was enough to buy sexual favours.

Khadroun, Mouhand and I were boys who had reached the age of sexual obsession. Frowning purposefully, Mouhand breathed through his lips as he counted, and I can still hear his sniffle; Khadroun however, is a mere whisper, an olive tree in disguise. Our biblical model requires a third person. I was the youngest and the shortest of the trio. But in appearance none of us seemed young. Boys age rapidly in the Moroccan climate. We had lost the softness prized by the imam and by the local young men of marriageable age. We had outgrown the knee of the imam, whose task was to teach us the Arabic alphabet and make us memorize verses of the Koran; the lap of his seldom spotless jellaba, which had once cushioned our rumps, had become the preserve of other lads, likewise with memories ready for jostling by his quiet ecstasy. For young men the time had come to devote attention to the opposite sex, in the marriage bed. Being exposed so early on to the urges of the body, it is hardly surprising that by the age of ten or twelve we fell victim to that insufferable itch.

Mouhand had a sister called Batoul, an early developer to put it mildly, whose bounteous bosom and lyrical hips had governed our dreams for some time. The rare touches that she allowed us (including her brother) were hopelessly elfin compared to the monstrosities we dreamed of. Our unforeseen stiffness was sublimated in obscene visions of Batoul's not entirely imaginary misconduct with Mouhand and our hopes of getting to grips with her ourselves – if only the world would have clemency and turn a blind eye while we borrowed time in a paradise of possibilities. I soon learned that erections take place in the mind.

The village was named after its landlord Bertollo, a sullen, bloated fellow whom we saw no more than once a month when he came to collect the rent. He would ride down the hill on his moped wearing a red crash helmet over his turban and muttering to himself – most probably some form of oral bookkeeping. He is the trusted extra in all my recollections of that remote village, and no doubt he still rides down the hill and will continue to do so for ages to come, amid the grieving olive trees, while the sunset presses a glaring kiss on the dome of his proud helmet.

It was a lively village, with its own idiot and mosque. It had a single tap to satisfy the needs of the entire population. Every day during the siesta Batoul squatted down by the tap and was invariably drawn into arguments about whose turn it was next. I can see her now, rising from her crouched position while the dispute grows all the more heated for being fanned by amusing female double entendres. Then Abdullah, a shaven-headed, unwashed boy from a family where all the boys are called Abdullah, a boy with a moustache and a nimbus of devoted flies, comes by astride his donkey (a skinny, mangy, docile animal), and gives Batoul's generous posterior a smack. Next he is bleeding from the nose (flies quiver on his upper lip): Mouhand cannot stand for such liberties with his virtuous sister to go unpunished. The rest of us watch. We, of course, have his permission, united as we are in our untapped potency, for which the female population would give thanks in due course.

Somewhere, in a corner of my memory that is in danger of overcrowding, Zalanbour shambles about wearing his eternal roll-neck sweater, humming a tune, a true children's friend, ever eager to offer initiation into the various functions of the male anatomy. As for his own, my memory tells me in uncertain terms that it was not to be sneezed at. And I was in a position to know. But he seems to have lost interest in me (I am eleven): all I get nowadays is a nod to our past complicity.

The roll-neck sweater was green. My memory, fired by the devilish impression he always made on me, would prefer to colour it red. The rippled eyebrows, the hairless face and body, and the ever bloodshot eyes with scimitars for lashes, the wide mouth: a Mephistopheles of hellish charm. He spoke with a tender, mesmerizing lisp. Since the time his mother had told him to get married instead of hanging around in the village all day, lines of worry had appeared on his forehead. I was a welcome guest at Zalanbour's house, where his mother would feed me sweetmeats and where I once heard him declare: 'I'm not hanging around. I have work on my hands.' He never raised his voice to his mother and always addressed her with lowered eyes. 'What kind of work then?' she asked, wiping my smeared lips (the chocolate was kept in a warm cupboard, alongside bins of flour and mouse droppings). Zalanbour took my hand, sat me on his right thigh and stroked the back of my head: 'You know, just work.' He had so often taken me on his rounds through the village and shown me his secret hiding places that his mother must have thought our constant companionship signalled a longing for fatherhood on his part. His favourite hideout was a hut on the hairy dwarf mountain beyond the village, where one winter night a pack of wolves interrupted our bonding ritual. Without displacing me from his altar he got up and went outside, pressing me against his belly with his right arm as if he were in the process of giving birth. The wolves fled and Zalanbour resumed his work standing. In times of dire need the shade of an olive tree sufficed. He would sit leaning against the trunk reading aloud from a pocket-sized Koran while I sat in the enclosure of his trousers, his spread knees, the unharvested olive trees, the resting donkey and the nibbling goat. From afar old men heard his recitation and waved approvingly. He always waved in return. Once I had to retrace our steps and search for his Koran, which had slipped from his hand in a moment of distraction. Should that Koran ever be found, there will be more than chocolate stains on certain pages to bear witness to our arcadian diversions. Moist, shady siestas.

I buried my thirty dirham behind our house: the open sesame to my first touch of woman. Remarks I had overheard under the night sky from young men debating the merits of the local fleshpots echoed in my mind. From the gloom of an unfamiliar backwater an invisible servant stepped forward to light my path: amongst mossy banks of darkness lay roseate womanhood. Batoul opened the cave. Udder-soft warmth. A profusion of images spiralled down to a single source: our neighbour's goat, which I had once studied with other-worldly fascination. Most important of all at this point was to conceal my inexperience with peremptory nonchalance. And especially not to let on that, in a sense, this was the first time. A smile in the dark.

Suddenly: 'Mama! Mama! I can't sleep: Hafid won't keep still!'

At long last I drifted into sleep, floating, dreaming, my hands still smarting from being slapped.

I had marked where the money was hidden with an oval stone. It had not escaped me that not a single round smooth stone behind our house was safe from hard-pressed squatters (mostly old men before evening prayer, sweeping the plain with a dispassionate stare and displaying a minimum of bare skin, usually no more than the shins — such are the advantages of a jellaba). The sunset greeted me with the smell of their drying faeces. My dwarfish stoop cast a giant's shadow as I hunted for the stone. Once the stone had been sighted, under a beetle, it gave a sign of recognition. I squatted for different reasons. The beetle, having got its breath back, resumed its Sisyphean labour. The soft throb of a moped wafted down the hillside. Wispy puffs of dust, the domed helmet a clown's red nose. There was a certain tingle in the twilight air, the horizon beamed with tender gratitude as after a salutary sneeze. The evening found us on the crest of the hill.

On our way down we came upon Abdullah on his donkey. The animal's flanks were heavily scarred. Mellowed now, like the fading light, Abdullah did no more than wave his stick. He parked the donkey behind his house, which was across the street from ours.

In order to get to town all we needed to do was follow the motorway that skirted the village. The street lights were, as usual, on strike. After half an hour's walk we arrived at the public gardens: a final swathe of night, thickly canopied, beyond which the city lights blinked festively. The moon made a collage of shadows on the pathway. A hunchback carrying two school satchels hobbled among the trees. We hid behind a bush. When he had dissolved into silence we set off again. We reached the fountain burbling wearily at the far end of the park. The flower beds nearby were dotted with empty plastic wine bottles, which filled the air with a stench that assumed human proportions as we approached the exit.

'Where are you going?' Zalanbour inquired. He stood leaning forward, his veined hands on his knees, his eyes popping with alcoholic tenderness.

We exchanged uneasy looks, shuffled our feet and made faces. Mouhand jingled the coins in his trouser pockets, possibly as a signal.

'Do you have money?' Zalanbour's eyebrows soared as if to make room for his face in close-up. He studied each of us in turn and then addressed Mouhand: 'Do you want to drink wine in town?'

I nodded, but Mouhand shook his head. He stated hoarsely what the money was for. Zalanbour's red face inflated like a balloon and split wide open in a guffaw. A hellish miasma emanated almost visibly from his mouth. Still chortling he gestured for us to follow him.

'I know something far better,' he mimed.

We were relieved, and gave each other significant, though meaningless nudges with our elbows. It was reassuring to have Zalanbour for our guide. If there was anyone who knew the underbelly of the town by heart, it was Zalanbour.

Zalanbour led the way down a maze of alleys, each with its distinctive shade of dusk. The streets were deserted except for a pack of emaciated mongrels which we warded off with stones. Finally Zalanbour stopped, turned to us unsteadily and extended his right hand.

'Give me the money and wait here.'

We handed him the money reluctantly. He knocked on a wooden door with a furtive air. Someone unbolted the door and he slipped inside. We shooed away two dogs and a cat. The door opened again and Zalanbour motioned us to step inside.

We made our way back through the park again. Mouhand leaned one hand against a tree and vomited so vigorously that his head crashed against the trunk. The drop that habitually pearled at the end of his nose (twitching left nostril, left corner of mouth curled) lengthened into a fluttering streamer. He cursed and gasped and clutched his belly with his left arm: one half was lit by the moon, the other half had melted into the trunk and dark foliage. I staggered about, convulsed with laughter. And Khadroun? I think I must have lost Khadroun somewhere in the dark. Perhaps there was no third person at all, perhaps I have split Mouhand up into different characters. And yet: on the crest of the hill I clearly saw three figures. I sense his presence constantly between my lines: Khadroun. I speak of 'us' as of a threesome.

We had been befuddled and belaboured – in that order. From the moment Zalanbour made me lie face down all I could do was let out smothered cries as I was transported back a few years into a room in Zalanbour's house: a sticky siesta, green roll-neck, shuttered windows. Mouhand was claimed by someone who appeared to be a stranger until a red helmet in the corner of the room gave him away. Mouhand's face was a mask of pain, his puffed out cheeks fighting back a spasm of retching. The sight of him made me laugh. So Zalanbour was still interested in me after all, and he was still his old gentle self. After a fluid finale he even wiped away the tinted afterflow with his hand. I turned over and sprawled languidly on my back, then reached out to take the last bottle of wine from the hand of Mouhand's rider. The stink from that smeared bottleneck was so overpowering that I was unable to quench my thirst. A gold tooth flashed at me triumphantly between grimaces. It was a touch humiliating to realize that both Zalanbour and his companion had been wearing nothing under their respective trousers and jellaba. One cancan kick was enough to send the skirt of a jellaba flying out of the way. In the solemnity of siesta moments it was fitting that our backs should be covered: we were and still are inclined towards undercover sodomy.

Mouhand kept complaining about the pain. I didn't stop laughing. Zalanbour had spent all our money on wine. Perhaps we could pay the goat another visit and thus revert to our rightful rung on the sexual ladder, I suggested to a spluttering Mouhand.

'I have a much better idea.'

Khadroun took shape among the leaves: a moonlit face. Being sufficiently sober, he led us home to the village without further comment. By the time we arrived I felt a stabbing pain in my loins, and not only from laughing.

Khadroun motioned us to be quiet and to wait for him on the crest of the hill. We went there and sat down under an olive tree. Mouhand rested his forehead on his drawn-up knees and muttered a prayer or an imprecation. Soon Khadroun turned up with Abdullah's donkey in tow, which he tied to the tree (requiring Mouhand to move over). I seem to remember him saying something about no more capers with goats. And letting his pants slide to the ground. With a gesture revealing practice he laid the tail over the croup. Standing on his toes he was at the right height to lean forward and grab hold of the ears. The donkey stared into space, shifted the croup and twitched a subcutaneous nerve. No sooner had Khadroun thrown back his straining torso (donkey and man united, a centaur is born) than Mouhand, miraculously recovered, pushed Khadroun out of his way. He laboured with passion and vigour, snorting, his mouth and nose twitching as always. A lengthening thread of slime dangled wildly from his nostril until it collapsed onto the donkey's croup.

Then it was my shadow's turn amid barely suppressed giggles to rest on the hands of Mouhand and Khadroun. A she-donkey. The moon was on our side: busy lice on the crest of the hill. We did not bother to walk our bride home afterwards, and fell into a contented sleep under the olive tree, side by side. Two weeks later Zalanbour vanished, the day before his wedding.

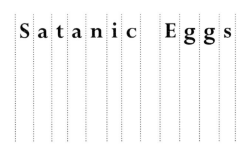

S a t a n i c   E g g s

The promulgation of the Law had far-reaching consequences in our cheerful village, too. Not only did our
two greengrocers, Sheik Badi ibn Djaan and Sheik
Abdullah, my father, see their trade decline, but also
our daily fare changed beyond recognition. We had
never realized that cucumbers and aubergines featured
so prominently in our diet. The villagers ate in discon-
tented silence, munching like children forced to con-
sume foul-tasting health foods. The salads had to forgo
their juicy refreshment. Our daily menu mourned the
loss of aubergine fried in olive oil with garlic and
parsley, aubergine stew with onions and more garlic
and parsley, aubergine stuffed with minced lamb and
tomato sauce and . . . garlic and parsley.

The imam consoled us in his Friday sermon with the

promise that our earthly privation would be liberally rewarded in Paradise: besides wine and sexual licence we would also enjoy cucumbers and aubergines to our hearts' content. Small comfort: undernourished imam, mouth-watering prayers.

In curtained rooms the women grieved, not so much over the injunction as over the discovery that had come too late. In their domestic innocence they had not known of all the uses to which those vegetables could be put. All they had ever done was chop them up to feed husbands and children.

The dreams of ripening girls began to take elongated shapes. I remember my sisters fast asleep, a smile playing on their lips which left no doubt as to the nature of the scenes unfolding behind their eyelids. And we slept side by side. Often I would wake up with a sisterly hand clasped around my risen loin-trophy. I was not the sort of boy to tell tales to my parents.

I think it was only the children, in their world of pink confectionary, who underwent the change without complaining.

Sheik Badi ibn Djaan and Sheik Abdullah sat on the stone mastaba in front of their vegetable stores, sadly smoking their nargilehs. Prior to the Law, they had enjoyed daily banter with veiled customers, they had indulged in the only extramarital contact with women they could afford. However briefly physical that contact may have been ('Your change, madam'), it was better than listening to Bertollo's escapades in dark wineshops and dens of delight.

Nowadays they saw no one but children with not enough money, who had to run back three times from shop to home (their ears burning redder each time), and forgetful men who always bought the wrong goods and whined about the prices. The two sheiks were so despondent they did not remonstrate when customers bargained the price down, and even handled the scales with painstaking accuracy.

'My wife – may Allah help you! – says that one kilo of potatoes – may Allah forgive you! – is not what it used to be. May Allah protect both you and us!'

Of course it was not the same. Unveil yourself and I have my pound of flesh. In other words: a peek down your bodice for me and some extra potatoes for you. Sheik Abdullah had known moments of mercenary poetry. But all that seemed centuries ago now.

'If you – may Satan not mislead us! – are not satisfied – Allah be praised! – why don't you go to town and buy from the townsfolk? May Allah protect us!'

Two portraits of Sheik Abdullah. Before the Law: a meek, frown-free forehead, a smoky chuckle reverberating in the bubble of his nargileh. After the Law: a wrinkled, haggard face, drained of all contentment. And thus a few months later Sheik Abdullah lay on his deathbed, with his pipe at his side.

In our village, where the only signs of political activity were the faded election posters on the walls of the mosque, we had always pictured the members of our venerable government as learned men who went about in Western-style suits and neckties and who spoke the language of the West. After the promulgation of the Law at the instigation of a spiritual leader, their appearance changed. The men suddenly grew imposing beards, their crowns sprouted turbans like icing extruding from a piping nozzle, their suits were discarded in favour of finely woven jellabas and they sat tailor-wise, speaking a high Arabic which they peppered with quotations from the Koran to lend weight to their political assertions.

As a rule, government announcements were slow to reach our village. This time it was different. One day, during the siesta, there was a sudden call for prayer. The muezzin made his summons with such strident insistence that even the old folk, for whom the siesta was sacred, were rudely awakened and made for the mosque without preliminary ablutions. The hungry dogs in the street froze, a hind leg poised in mid-air to scratch behind an ear, and let out inquisitive yelps; women and girls stopped their scouring and rolled down their sleeves; even the flies swarming around the refuse dump seemed to slow down in puzzlement. The children, who never slept during the afternoon rest anyway, ceased their fumblings and leapt out of bed, whooping.

It was, of course, the imam who told us the news. He stood on the minbar with his staff at his side and read out the declaration. He wore an expression of grave sadness. The good men of our government had long been striving to curb wantonness and loose behaviour, especially among women, who were most susceptible to the nefarious influences menacing Moslems. The government was vigorously engaged in abolishing every activity or object that might excite the female imagination. A major decision had now been reached: the first of many that would follow. For reasons that did not require further explication, it was henceforth forbidden for women to either purchase or handle cucumbers and aubergines. They were to be banned from the market. And may Allah bless our Prophet and his descendants, may He bring peace to all Moslems and safeguard them against the ruses of Satan and his demons. Amen.

Amen, the crowd responded in unison, after which everyone left the mosque and went home quietly. No one spoke. Children who broke into a playful salvo were immediately silenced with a cane and dragged home by the ear. When my father, Sheik Abdullah, came home, he reclined on his wooden divan and lit his nargileh. As he did not say a word to my mother, she ran to the woman next door to hear the news.

This marked the beginning in our village – and in the whole country – of a stifled tension, the likes of which we had only experienced previously during Ramadan. The men were resigned, saying that the wisdom of our government was beyond all doubt and may Allah help us. At first the women resolved, as a quiet form of protest, to boycott the vegetable shops. This gave rise to nutritional and marital chaos in every household, and the women decided to terminate their action. I think they understood, with the foresight typical of women, that the prohibition-crazed government would seize on their protest as an excuse to impose further bans.

Their unanimous return to their former tasks (which was reported in the papers) was, however, something my father Sheik Abdullah did not live to see. A few days before this event he had withdrawn from wife and children to rest on his divan with his nargileh, as he did every day after work. He no longer perused his Koran. Behind his closed door the bubbling of his nargileh reassured us, until one day the throttle of smoke in water fell silent. It was some time before my mother dared enter his room. My father's lifeless body was still lying in the same position, the tip of the nargileh still resting in his drooling mouth; only his turban had slipped askew. It turned out that he had not taken food for several weeks.

After a month of mourning I took charge of Sheik Abdullah's business. Under the kindly watchful eyes of my neighbour Sheik Badi ibn Djaan, I made a habit of sitting out in front of the mastaba to smoke my water pipe. The vegetables and fruits were kept inside crates in the shady interior of the shop. I sat in the barred shade of a straw awning. At the back of the shop there was a small alcove with a straw mat, on which my father used to take his siesta. There were two niches in the alcove with dusty, disused oil lamps.

Most of the day was taken up with smoking and watching the world go by. Sheik Badi ibn Djaan was visited every day by the same wrinkled, toothless old men, whose purpose was to talk, never to buy. They sat on their heels in the shade and mumbled a hodgepodge of words which became less intelligible the more I smoked. Now and then they would unwind their turbans and stroke their purple-veined, knobbly pates. My contribution to the discourse was restricted to the occasional smile of understanding or a murmured prayer in response to their invocations.

Like all the older men who came past, they held up the hem of their jellaba. Some leaned on a staff, rough and withered as themselves, while they warded off unwelcome flies with unsteady hands; their eyes were watery and sad, but still alert to the sight of a woman, whereupon they braced their scrawny shoulders. I was a wellspring of youth beside the summer drought of those venerable old men.

It was always a pleasure to be of service to the veiled women. The burqa, a veil that reaches from the nose to the breasts, gave each woman, regardless of her age, a certain forbidden charm. I was happy to shake off my torpor and would try to prolong their stay with witticisms and mercurial sales talk. The sight of young hands fumbling under the burqa for the purse tucked in the bosom continued to throb in my sluggish veins for a long time. Behind the veil the throat and collarbones were bare. I believe the women were not entirely unaware of the effect of their tinkling bangles and heavily kohled eyes. A mere glimpse of the infinitely tender shadowy cleft between their straining breasts, where the purse was secreted, warranted an extra pound of merchandise. When asked to taste a melon they would raise the veil briefly, all too often displaying a ripe mouth lavishly treated with cosmetic herbs and pigments. It was always worth the effort. I began to understand my father, Sheik Abdullah.

I spent the siesta in the alcove. I lay on the straw mat, which still dreamed of my father's right side, and smoked. Daydreams offered a parade of intimate femininities, blow-ups of flesh and images of women performing elaborate ablutions before prayer. I was, indeed I am, technically speaking, still a virgin. With cupped hands they scooped up water to . . . and suddenly the water turned into something else, something that had been ousted from our lives for months: a cucumber, an aubergine, and it was some time before I felt the iron ring under the mat press into my back.

The alcove was not much smaller than the cell where I now spend shabby days in the company of four others, but it was cooler. Our daily fare consists of white beans, which unleash a veritable war among us at night, when we lie packed together with barely enough room to breathe. I entertain the men with stories about the alcove and what went on there. Without a nargileh. Yesterday there was a great commotion on the square before the mosque. Ecstatic ululation reached our cell.

My green and deep purple evocations rouse the stunned spirits of my cell-mates. One night when I was awakened it was not by a hard tumescence nosing between the folds of my flesh, but by a gob of spittle landing on my cheek: the lecher had wanted to spit in his hand to ease entry, but had missed his mark in the gloom.

Every morning at cock's crow I went to my shop. The muezzin called for prayer in a voice cracking with emotion. Men entered the mosque in pairs, forgoing both coffee and voiding of the bowels. Young girls made their way to the green pump with buckets and pitchers. Children yelled, children ran to the Koran school turning their slates this way and that like steering wheels. I had to throw stones to drive them away; they had a pathological urge to insult everyone and their mother in the foulest language, which they had picked up God knows where. Yet another rascal skips by, excoriating me for the wanton behaviour of my innocent mother. A stone hits the back of his head and he raises his hand to the pain as he runs moaning into the mosque, where another punishment awaits him. But there are more children in my path than stones, it seems. When I finally arrive at my destination Sheik Badi ibn Djaan has, as usual, already opened his shop, made a pot of tea and filled his water pipe with bhang.

Sheik Badi ibn Djaan was nicknamed Abou Ftila, Father Wick, by the children. He wore a yellowed, sweat-stained skullcap that had a little tuft in the centre like the wick of a candle. His long greying beard was streaked with henna. From time to time he would wrap strips of cotton around his henna-soaked beard to fix the dye. He had a lisp and a huge gold tooth. Under his impressive nose (strawberry pores and a tracery of varicose veins) his upper lip was shaven, and his ears were likewise majestically proportioned. He did not say much and when he did speak the lisp made him unintelligible. I wonder how long it took the police to get the gist of his statement. His deep-set eyes were ringed with the kind of creases that intimate benevolence. I should not have allowed those eyes to deceive me; I should never have trusted those ears, either.

I greeted him and sat down by his side. He poured me a glass of tea and I prepared my nargileh. It must have been the end of the month, because Bertollo, the landlord of the village, was riding his moped from one house to the next to collect the rent. He parked his vehicle in front of the shop and sat down with us. He mopped his forehead with a handkerchief but did not take off the crash helmet he wore on top of his turban. There was a marked resemblance between his helmet and his portly figure. Sheik Abou Ftila poured him some tea. Bertollo slurped the hot tea and launched into a tirade about his tenants and how they were not to be trusted. He kept sighing and mopping his brow.

When he had stuffed our rent into his moneybag he emptied his glass and got up to go, turning to me with the words: 'Your father was a good man.' We saw him call at a few more houses and when he was out of sight we could still hear the puffing and coughing of his old moped as it grew faint in the distance. No doubt he would celebrate his bulging moneybag tonight by drowning his sorrow at the loss of a man like my father.

At the call for midday prayer Sheik Abou Ftila stood up, closed his shop and headed for the mosque, holding up the hem of his jellaba. I stayed behind, and by the time the muezzin had come to the end of his summons the street was empty. It was Friday and the sermon was sure to be lengthy. The shadows were shortening. A donkey brayed from afar and a goat bleated in reply. A child was crying in a house nearby, there was some motherly scolding, too. My eyelids drooped. The buzz of the moped returned, then receded again. I grinned at the idea of Bertollo having forgotten one of his tenants and pictured the happy family being roused by the belated knock on the door, and fell asleep.

She walked off swaying her hips affectedly, a minuet of pert buttocks. She had drawn her black haïk tight around her body. She did not wear a veil. I took the image of her face – a palette of crimson and hazel and fairness of complexion untouched by the sun – and her hips with me to the alcove and emptied my loins of a welcome impulse. The pockets of a jellaba are just two slits in the sides, no more.

I do not know how long she had stood before me when I opened my eyes at last. The streets were still deserted; the Friday sermon was still under way. She took her time deciding what to buy and asked if she might pay me tomorrow. But of course. I helped her wrap her purchases. Her haïk slipped down from her head over her shoulders and she did not take the trouble to readjust it. Her jewellery was of cheap gold, it seemed to me, and her neck of the costliest skin imaginable. Under her rosy earlobes her jawline was silky with transparent down.

'*Ya sittí*, my damsel,' I said, 'you can pay me – may Allah protect us from avarice – at your convenience – may Allah show no mercy to the miser.'

Holding her straw basket in her left hand, she pulled the haïk over her head with her right and salaamed. She walked off swaying her hips affectedly, a minuet of pert buttocks. She had drawn her black haïk tight around her body. She did not wear a veil. I took the image of her face – a palette of crimson and hazel and fairness of complexion untouched by the sun – and her hips with me to the alcove and emptied my loins of a welcome impulse. The pockets of a jellaba are just two slits in the sides, no more.

I lay on my back, spent, and spread my arms in the ebbing of my solitary lust. I took her with me into the gloaming behind my closed eyelids, but my loins granted me no rest and I fed their greed with liberal hand. Only after the stalwart finally rested his head on my belly, felled at last, did I notice that there was something under the straw mat pressing into my back. I slid the mat away and saw a small trapdoor with an iron ring in the middle. I raised the hatch and in the space below stood a crate and in that crate – but Sheik Abou Ftila was calling my name and I hurried outside. Needless to say I replaced the mat first.

A yellowish gleam from the guard's office penetrates our cell, evoking the days of oil lamps in the niches of my alcove at the back of my vegetable shop.

After Friday evening prayer and supper at home (white beans with chicken and parsley) I return to my vegetable shop to inspect my find. The street is dotted with young men sitting in little groups smoking, their fiery cigarette tips like so many Argus eyes. As I pass by they give me a friendly *salaamaleikum*. A crackling radio plays nondescript music, becoming weaker as the batteries run down. A bottle of wine is handed round; I decline and walk on – in the past.

I lit the oil lamps and prepared my nargileh. Portentous shadows danced on the walls of the alcove. I pulled away the mat, opened the hatch and put an oil lamp by the hole in the floor. Then I sat against the wall and lit my pipe. The alcove became a forest of erotic forms with lascivious demons lurking in the shadows; the walls were breathing. The nargileh had all the stateliness of a risen member, the niche seemed to be made of flesh. The oil lamps licked the walls with satyr-tongues. I got out the crate and studied the contents at length, with restrained veneration.

'They're beautiful,' she whispered. She extended a trembling hand, then paused and opened the damp palm as in supplication.

She had not paid yet. She came to me again on Saturday during the midday prayer, and I asked if she would take tea with me in the alcove. She glanced round, wearing the same haïk as before, and nodded unabashed. I collected glasses, teapot and a tray from Sheik Badi ibn Djaan's shop, and took them with me. After bolting the door of my shop I invited her to sit on the straw mat. She slipped her haïk off her head, with the kind of sigh that appears to be the statutory accompaniment to that gesture.

The pot rose, bent over and poured tea into our glasses. The nargileh lifted its snout and placed the tip between my lips. It started bubbling. The glasses floated up to our mouths and tilted to let us drink, after which they returned to the tray, in a silent repetitive ritual.

She sat down on the straw mat and crossed her legs beneath a profusion of folds, while the iron ring under the blissful burden of her splayed seat must have been recast in a different shape.

I said there was no problem – Allah preserve your beauty, *sitti* – if she paid me the next day – Inshallah! I said her beauty could not but inspire confidence in me – may Allah forbid that we lose trust in our fellow

Moslems. I said I had not seen her before in the village. I said I could barely control myself and could I kiss her?

She leaned forward to reach me a kiss, but was interrupted by a frown: she said there was something under the mat that was hurting her.

Perhaps it was my intoxication that induced me to show her what was in the crate. More probably, though, it was a declaration of love, a way to reel her in with my heartstrings.

I opened the hatch and brought up the crate. A sob convulsed her breast when she set eyes on the two shiny aubergines and three glorious cucumbers lying in the crate. Her mouth fell open.

'They're beautiful,' she whispered. She extended a trembling hand, then paused and opened the damp palm in supplication.

I flicked my hand from the wrist in an inviting gesture and she ran her forefinger slowly, caressingly, over the smooth plumpness of the aubergine, the ridged skin of the cucumber. Then she took the cucumber, like a sacred object, in her right hand and the aubergine, like a rare egg, in her left.

I did not understand what her motives were – I was younger then and could not imagine what women did in their forbidden boudoirs, the same boudoirs I now visit daily in my dreams – that is to say, if I am not disturbed by my cell-mates' taunts. I am the youngest here and badly need my elbow. I should never have told all those stories.

She lowered her head to brush her lips over each one in turn. My lust throbbed under my jellaba. Lost in her ecstatic indolence she did not notice the spasm that passed through my body – but there was the voice of Sheik Badi ibn Djaan, and gone was the magic, the dream, the torment.

Sheik Badi ibn Djaan wanted to know if I had borrowed his teapot and glasses. Yes, I had.

'Why don't you ever go to the mosque for prayer?' he inquired when I returned his tray with the tea things. She was still in the alcove, her hands – and who knows, not only her hands – full. I had signalled to her not to make a sound.

'You're not a child any more,' he lisped as he took the tray from me, staring at the two glasses. 'May Allah keep Satan at bay – your poor father – may Allah have mercy on him – was a good man. There can be no good fortune without the mercy of God, and prayer is the prime duty of each Moslem. A good Moslem does not die if he dies in the shadow of a son. It is unseemly that you have ceased praying for his soul and that you, as his only son, are not following his good example. Your poor mother – may Allah forgive me – is a good woman. She still wears black, which is more than you can say of most widows these days. May you be a good son – with Allah's protection – to your poor mother.'

He also had a tendency to stammer. He averted his eyes during his monologue and I said that Allah – inshallah – would surely show me the path of righteousness. He nodded and withdrew into his shop, his sail-like ears red and almost transparent in the glaring sun.

Her name was Quthaa. I wonder if she was worth going to prison for. Of course I could not imagine, segregated as I was from other girls except my sisters, what the local girls (when they were not scrubbing, fetching water, cooking, washing dishes) got up to in their boudoirs. Indeed I could not imagine them having any spare time left after their chores. Perhaps our blessed government was right after all: what else could such perversions be but the work of Satan? It is and was essential to secure the purity of women, in both body and mind. Perhaps it was the influence of the West. The fact that I could tolerate certain spectacles at all I now impute to my youthful eagerness.

How else could I have countenanced that green between shadowy moss and pallid thighs? No sooner had Sheik Abou Ftila retreated into his shop than I hastened back to the alcove. There was a strange, moist dementia in her eyes as she craned her neck and whispered, begging me to kiss her. She darted a cold tongue into my mouth.

The call for evening prayer was already sounding when she readjusted her clothing, her eyes downcast. She drew the haïk over her head and languidly made her exit. I wiped the tip of the cucumber and put the crate away. With aching calves and drenched jellaba I filled my nargileh and drifted into sleep in the

alcove. I was – Allah help us all – not older than
seventeen.

At home I took to sleeping alone.

After two days she came back, this time chaperoned
by an old woman. It was, of course, time for midday
prayer. The chaperon gave me a knowing look as if we
had met before. Her face was a spider's web of wrinkles, her lips seemed in danger of being swallowed up
by her mouth. The women did their shopping and
paid their debt. The old woman handed me the money
and said: '*Yabní* – my son – aren't you going to invite
us for tea?'

At first the quaky witch was merely an observer. She
was so agitated by what she saw that her heavy panting
soon turned into neighing. She began to shake so
violently that her contours were barely discernible.
She could no longer control herself. First she tried the
cucumber, but the aubergine proved more suited to
her falham. There they lay, jerking and heaving in
shameless abandon, while in the mosque the true
believers knelt and prostrated themselves in a different
act of worship. The poor chaperon, for all her desicca-
tion, discharged an indeterminate fluid. The tremors
of old age had apparently blurred the distinction
between bladder and womb.

The old chaperon may have been her mother or
grandmother; in any case she was the first to pay for
the cucumbergine delights, which gave me the idea of
charging for these favours in future. The next day

Quthaa brought along one of her sisters, and then another: the village turned out to be blessed with more women than I had ever imagined. She brought along her friends, too – no doubt the same girls she quarrelled with every day over who was next in line for the village pump. Their shared lusty appetite evidently cleared the air. They always came in pairs (to avoid arguments) and always during the hour of midday prayer, a time that always struck me as the least suitable for expending impatient loins.

I remember a woman who refused to remove her veil, but who parted the flesh of her shame unblushingly before my eyes. Another insisted that I leave the alcove: I charged her extra. One woman, who prided herself on her experience, had her way with two cucumbers at once and I had to enlist Quthaa's help in extracting them. Quthaa's suggestion to bite a piece off did not find favour with her friend.

And all that time, by Allah, I did not venture inside any of these women. Our ritual was autistic. The one time Quthaa requested my entry via the aperture resembling a small crater (a sunburst of lines, an aureole of brownish shadow) – just that one time I satisfied her demand, and only because the flesh got the better of me, while her green sceptre, which was beginning to look as wrinkled as her chaperon (from hard work), remained in place.

After she had taken her leave with some demurral, I had to clean the floor and mat of the seepage of their lechery. They walked away on tottering legs, exhausted, and not infrequently they embraced each other afterwards, weeping with joy. It saddened me that they gave me so minor a role to play in their bliss. Quthaa's request was not repeated. So I decided to double the prices: the spirit of commerce took possession of me, turning profit into my main gratification.

With the exception of Quthaa every visitor had to pay. For three dirham I permitted the women to view the crate; the price of touching or kissing the fetish was fifteen dirham. Those wishing to explore their innermost depths had to hand over thirty dirham.

After a while I had earned an enormous sum of money. At home we could now afford pigeon stuffed with rice, pistachio, almonds and raisins and braised with onions, garlic and parsley. The pigeons were caught for us by a retarded lad in the village, whom I paid well. Now and then I bought a lamb which I slaughtered myself, even though it was not the season for sacrifice. Decadence held sway in our home. My sisters flaunted their expensive headscarves, my mother wore handwoven garments. I pretended to her that the shop was doing exceptionally well. I bought a Western-style outfit complete with tie and shirt, although my mother said such clothing did not suit me. I bought a radio and even a television, which I connected to a car battery as our village lacked electricity. After supper we would watch every single programme; my favourite was a series about a cigar-smoking detective with tousled hair and a long crumpled raincoat (I wanted to buy the same coat) who drove a similarly crumpled car and who solved crimes – he would have found a valuable ally in Abou Ftila. We even watched the news, which was read out in a language we did not understand.

In the alcove we tried to be as discreet as we could, but perhaps Abou Ftila did not always go to the mosque for prayer, or if he did he must have left his ears behind at his shop.

I will cease these evocations. Here in this cell, which is filthier than the crimes I am accused of, they have not stood me in good stead. Last night I cried out in my sleep and woke one of the guards who, surprisingly, did not demand retribution for the satyric trespasses that had already reached their triumphant conclusion. He grinned, flashed a gold tooth, and slapped his club against the palm of his hand, the way I had seen prison guards do on screen before television was banned.

I yearn for my village with Bertollo on his moped; I miss the boredom and the hidden mischief, the somniferous calm of the nargileh, the women bustling about and the shrill voices of the children, the godliness and the blistering sun during midday prayer.

I cannot remember when the two gendarmes came to arrest me. I know it was on the day I had planned to go to town to buy myself a long raincoat. The gendarmes were like two peas in a pod. They had Lebanese curly moustaches, savage eyes and the kind of squared shoulders that go with law enforcement. Prior to being handcuffed I received the statutory trouncing. They beat the daylights out of me: a fitting farewell to my dusky alcove. The two men gripped me by the elbows and led me to their car. They nodded to Abou Ftila, who mumbled *salaamaleikum* and went on smoking his pipe unperturbed. I was taken to the police station in town. It was the first time I saw the inside of a car.

My mother followed us weeping hysterically, going down on her knees to plead with the immutable judiciaries, rolling over the ground, showering Sheik Abou Ftila with mother-and-hell imprecations. She was restrained by the imam. The old men stood about in front of the mosque, waiting. My sisters did not leave the house; they peeped out from behind half-closed shutters, like the other women.

Quthaa and her accomplices were arrested, too. The poor chaperon succumbed to a heart attack when the gendarmes burst into her house. One of her sisters stabbed a knife into her pregnant belly (the child, which I picture as a cucumber with arms and feet, would not see the light of the village). The rest of the women, unveiled, bare-headed, tore their hair out, watched in silence by the fly-ridden children standing hollow-backed, belly-button-bared, wide-eyed, unshod, snotty-nosed, a fidgety hand in the cleft of their buttocks. The dogs had fled. And all the while Abou Ftila sat and smoked his pipe, weighing a moneybag in his left hand – indeed, his left hand.

In the courtroom we were locked into cages, one for

me and the other for the women. My mother, who could not control her sobbing and pleading, was ushered outside. Among those present were the twin gendarmes, arms proudly crossed over their broad chests; their moustaches curled in a cruel smile. All eyes were fixed on us, filled with scorn and also, Allah help me, with some measure of envy.

The Kadi bore a strong resemblance to my father. White-bearded, black-turbaned, scrawny, haggard, he had a large yellow-leaved book before him, which he did not consult although the frown on his forehead suggested hard-earned erudition, as did his towering turban. The burden of other people's sins had given his narrow shoulders a permanent slope. His hoarse voice had a touch of weariness.

It was intolerable, he said, that such misdeeds went on in a society which did all in its power – and no doubt with ultimate success – to banish the influence of Satan. It was intolerable that such despicable acts, the sight of which caused the Angels to shed their feathers, should go unpunished. In the name of Allah and the Sharia the women would be borne across the town on camels, they would be stoned, spat upon, humiliated and cursed by the townsfolk. Then they would be put to death. Taking my young age into consideration the Kadi condemned me to twenty years' imprisonment.

Yesterday there was a great commotion on the square before the mosque. Ecstatic ululation reached our cell. The women, or what was left of them, were strung up and, judging by the pandemonium, the entire population must have been in attendance. I overheard two guards telling each other how some inquisitive children had been looking up the skirts of the dangling women, and how their mothers had dragged them away by their ears, and I thought of the children in my village and how they made a dash for the girls bending over the pump, peeped up their skirts and dodged a box on the ears, all in one sweeping sally.

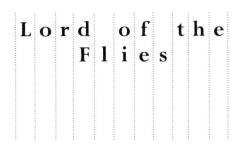

Lord of the Flies

With Zalanbour's return our village was visited by demons, who moved in with the family of the late Sheik Abdullah. It is common knowledge that djinns prefer to reside in a well, and it was indeed there that the family first became aware of their presence.

Life in the village seemed to be following its expected course: I had started praying in the mosque and Mouhand had found work and a wife. Khadroun rustled among the olive trees as ever. But judging by the behaviour of our village elders and the children (the two best gauges of unforeseen change) there was something afoot. The sheiks became taciturn and spent even more time at the mosque than before, while their toothless utterances, ever sparse, were now devoted exclusively to prophylactic prayer. The children grew increasingly boisterous and plaintive.

In generous moods I sometimes bought sweets for my youngest sister Fatima, six years old and a little masterwork of ringlets, vivacity and enchantment. But when I handed her the pink goodies she snatched them from me, and when I told her in jest that I deserved a hug by way of thanks she began to cry, flung them down and ran to my mother: 'Mama! Mama! Hafid has thrown my sweets on the floor!'

And our imam took to drink.

Naturally the faithful did not, could not, know that the unsteadiness of our imam, in gait and sermon, was caused by wine. Beneath his spotless jellaba his legs buckled as if he might pass out at any moment. Now and then he would let out a weak laugh at some phrase ('the good Moslem – may Allahahaha hahahahave mercy on us!') but this did not distract the congregation from their methodical harkening. He was a man who prided himself on two pilgrimages to Mecca and a dark stain on his forehead from praying.

When the drone during morning prayer grew too loud he patted his turban wearily saying that Allah was everywhere, there was no point in shouting as He would hear anyhow. A good believer prays in silence. If you please.

Khadroun, Mouhand and I were still in the habit of communing with our shadows on the crest of the hill. This time Abdullah accompanied us. The sun was sinking behind the hairy shanks of the mountain overlooking our village. Since his wedding Mouhand avoided mentioning sex; all he spoke of nowadays was his work and the children he would have. Khadroun's rustling was barely audible.

Young, unwashed, Abdullah told us amid a chorus of flies that not a day went by without him hearing things move in the well at their house. The only time he had screwed up enough courage to take a look he had seen the water heave as if something was trying to get out. He swore on the Koran that he had also heard voices. Since then he refused to go anywhere near it. 'I always knew water was dangerous,' he concluded with a wise frown.

We jeered at his story – of course, he was just inventing excuses for his unwashed state. He went away humiliated, sobbing quietly and dabbing the bloody nose Mouhand had given him.

After a while Mouhand stood up, shook out his jellaba, salaamed and headed home, while I and the gathering dusk stayed behind. One of the olive trees started moving. I thought it was Khadroun. But it was someone who had been hiding behind him and who now stole ahead, then stopped and looked round, as if startled to find that the tree was not following behind. He stole away with a great show of self-effacement, and in his eagerness for invisibility the shadowy figure tripped over the hem of his jellaba, then scrambled to his feet again and ran off towards the mountain, holding up his hem with his hand.

Evidently Abdullah was not the only one to have heard noises in the well. Soon his mother Fatima came to tell my mother about the misfortunes that had befallen them: she feared for her little ones, she could not sleep at night. She swore by the Koran and the Prophet that she had heard a voice cry for help in the well. She could not possibly stay at her house any longer. My mother was supportive as usual.

So the late Sheik Abdullah's family moved out of their house and into ours. Until such time as the imam had driven out the djinns, mother Fatima and her numerous offspring would stay with us.

And her offspring were truly numerous. She had one son, the unwashed Abdullah, and many daughters, all of them named Fatima, whose exact number I never ascertained, so that it seemed as if not even widowhood had put an end to Fatima's procreation.

The poor woman was filled with trepidation and dread. To my mother she bewailed the loss of her son, Abdullah the martyr, and of her other son, Abdullah, who had been put in prison, and of her husband, Sheik Abdullah, who had died, for she had known only misfortune and grief since.

And while she was about it she added a jeremiad (slapping her hands on her vast lap) about the chickens and the goat they had left behind, and how they would be set upon by the predatory djinns. I hoped she did not notice I was grinning.

I was to go to her house and fetch the animals, horned and combed, in the company of the imam. And as I shut the door behind me on my way to the imam, I heard mother Fatima say: 'I am ashamed of my only remaining son Abdullah, the scamp, the good-for-nothing. Where is he when I need him? What have I done to deserve this?'

I found the imam squatting for pressing business behind our house. My *salaamaleikum* startled him out of his diuretic concentration; oddly enough he looked caught out. I explained my mission and his face lit up with relief. Leaning on my shoulder he said: 'You know, you always were my best pupil at the Koran school. I shall go with you, indeed I shall – wait. May it please Allah to grant this village more of the likes of you.'

When we entered Sheik Abdullah's house (left foot first), we could hear the sound of slobbering coming from the well, as if the djinns were guzzling an unclean meal. Abdullah was right. '*Bismillah,*' the imam muttered. Under the thatch roof we found the chickens roosting and the goat munching, unperturbed. The chickens squawked with housewifely displeasure when I grabbed them by their legs, but the goat just went on chewing and followed behind meekly, as if to acknowledge our juvenile intimacy.

The imam went to the well, held his palms together book-wise and began whispering a sura from the Koran. The water in the well rose up, churning and bubbling furiously. The imam ended his recitation, but the water did not quieten.

It was dusk by the time the imam and I returned with the chickens and the goat. The imam hurried to the mosque for prayer and I hurried along with him. He conducted the prayer in a hurry, too.

After evening prayer I saw Abdullah, who avoided my eye like a shamed child. When I reached the crest of the hill Mouhand was not there – but the shadowy shape flitting from tree to tree was.

During morning prayer we waited in vain for the imam to appear. The eldest member of the congregation had to be persuaded to take his place and lead us in prayer. At first he coyly affected reluctance, but when another elder protested that we didn't have all day (which we did have) and that if it took much longer he would do the job himself, the old man made for the mihrab with remarkable agility for someone his age and commenced the prayer.

The same elder also conducted the noon prayer. Afterwards I called at the imam's house, but my knock was not answered. I came home to find mother Fatima driving her son Abdullah out of the kitchen with a stick. The chickens took flight, the children roared with laughter, the children yelled, the goat chewed.

By the pump two girls were pulling each other's hair out, while an old woman, a shrivelled scrap of life, crouched down to fill her pitchers, shaking her head sadly. One of the girls was Batoul, Mouhand's sister. A tear in her blouse revealed a large portion of her quaking, overripe bosom, which was the colour of coffee the way I liked it: not too milky. She lunged at the cheeks of her adversary with blind claws.

In all the houses short-tempered mothers scolded their whining children. Dogs barked and howled, a donkey brayed in the distance. A gust of wind blew dust and fetor from the refuse heap. Everything signalled that the hour of siesta was upon us.

After the fifth prayer I knocked on the imam's door again. It was some time before he appeared. With nervous gestures and a timid shake of the head he let me in.

His dwelling revealed a dearth of feminine order: practical and nondescript, the few items of furniture disposed according to the erratic rules of immediate convenience. He was wearing his grey jellaba and had slung the tapering end of his white turban around his neck.

Before I had time to speak he laid his hand on my shoulder and asked: 'Can I trust you?'

To avoid the eyes of evening strollers our shades flitted from olive tree to olive tree. The imam, his head covered with the hood of his jellaba, held my hand. On the crest of the hill we waited under Khadroun's shadowy protection until nightfall before hurrying to the mountain where Zalanbour was expecting us.

His roll-neck sweater had turned red. He had always been a man of muted exuberance, his mild charm did not allow for the seethings and eruptions of passion. His tenderness had grown even more malleable: the temples of his languid elegance had whitened over the years. His nodding smile told me that his return to the village would have far-reaching consequences. He and Bertollo, the village landlord, were sitting by a fire surrounded by bottles of wine. He sat like a prophet, dignified and beardless.

His sexual propensity had likewise been prophetically resolved: his fondness for boys was a thing of the past. He sought no favours from me.

The imam and I started drinking, and it was long past midnight when we made our way home, reeling and staggering and trying to make as little noise as possible.

Our house groaned wearily under the snoring burden of our guests. There were children sleeping everywhere, including the open courtyard. My mother and the widow Fatima were asleep in the kitchen.

Having tiptoed into the house with drunken discretion, I could not find anywhere to sleep. I heard a stifled flurry coming from the room where my sisters slept. I glanced inside and the flurry subsided, but there were flies circling over the space between my two sisters: it was Abdullah, pretending to be asleep. I shook him awake and pulled him out by his ear. Suppressed panic gave his eyes an imploring look.

I dragged him outside and aimed several kicks at the rigid zipper of his unwashed trousers. The flies returned from their temporary flight to settle on his blood after I left him behind, crumpled around his lynchpin, groaning, reeking.

Once Bertollo was well and truly drunk during one of Zalanbour's nocturnal debauches, this crash-helmeted homunculus lost all sense of decency. He would gyrate towards me, bill and coo, purse his lips, and pull my clothes about until a look from Zalanbour froze his carnal tribute. Then he would take a bottle of wine and sit cross-legged, a paragon of respectable composure.

It was clear that Zalanbour no longer brooked sodomy in his presence.

Bertollo, crestfallen, let his lower lip sag. There was an oddly sanctimonious quality about Zalanbour's renunciation of his earlier penchant.

I had the feeling something was missing in our house. When a house has been cleaned, the spirit of former chaos blows through the new order, evoking a sense of omission – that was what I had felt for the last few days.

Of course. The flies. Abdullah's mother Fatima slapped her thighs, wailing that her son had most certainly been abducted by demons. Fatima always had something to grieve over, it seemed. She was a woman born to lose.

Since the night I had given him that well-deserved beating, Abdullah had vanished. Naturally I did not mention my disciplinary action: if Fatima had got wind of it she would undoubtedly have had a seizure.

If the imam did not purge her house of the djinns at once she would die, she said. That very night. The imam was to commence the ritual exorcism the same night, in my presence.

First we went to Zalanbour for some Dutch courage. By the third bottle we felt reckless. After that we teetered to Fatima's house. The streets were deserted. Suddenly we heard windows shutting warily: our laughter was evidently taken for the laughter of demons.

The imam stood by the well and recited the requisite verses with a lot of stammurmuring and amnesiac frowning, while I posted myself by the door. I could hardly keep my eyes open and must have nodded off – I know I did because I woke up with a start to find that the imam had gone. I do not know what his ritual entailed, nor what sort of forces, demonic or natural, he was up against, but the poor imam's motionless body was lodged in the well, his bare feet sticking out of the water; he had left his sandals behind on the ground. I was at great pains to persuade Mouhand to help me get the imam out of the well.

The imam's lifeless body was laid out by two village elders. A door served as the bier. The whole village joined the procession to the graveyard; there was a crush of people wanting to touch the bier or to help carry it. The village elders intoned a shrill, grating dirge.

Fatima had yet another reason to grieve: this was the last straw. She was at the end of her tether, and lay sick in bed moaning and wailing, sobbing and weeping.

The villagers sealed up the well and tore down her house. At dusk the children played among the ruins and went home to supper covered in bruises and bumps.

'Look,' said Mouhand, pointing from the crest of the hill to the pale mountain top. For a brief moment, a darkly seething mass could be seen aside the mountain. We waited for it to reappear, but the horizon remained immaculate.

With a sigh of routine husbandhood, Mouhand said his supper was waiting for him and set off for home. I stayed behind with – no, Khadroun had become an olive tree once more.

Our new imam was a small scaramouch with a hunched back, who invariably carried two school satchels. The village elders had found him praying under a palm tree somewhere, and his devotion and pious diction had moved them. He had responded to their appeals with a lengthy discourse on modesty, the prime virtue of Moslems, and the necessity of leadership in Islam, all the while maintaining that he personally was too lowly for imamhood – only to accede in the end.

His misshapenness and the benevolence that was written in every line of his walnut face made him a likely candidate for holiness. The whole village spoke of him with awe. When he went past the women beside the village pump he would pull the hood of his jellaba down over his eyes; he spoke pacifying words to warring children in the street and dealt only rare and feeble blows with the cane during Koran lessons – so feeble as to give the fathers cause for concern.

He refused to lodge with one of the village elders: 'The mosque, the *Baitallah*, the House of God, is where I belong,' he said. At these words tears welled in the elders' eyes. They could hardly wait for him to die so that they might pray for him at his tomb. For the time being they had to be content with doing so behind his back.

He slept in the mosque, using the two satchels for a pillow. He and his two satchels were inseparable. The children at the Koran school gazed admiringly and dreamy-eyed at the satchels, but no one was permitted a look inside. The children began to whine that they wanted to go away to school, much to the chagrin of their mothers, who abhorred the city.

All in all this hunchbacked troll, reverently known as Abou Hadba, Father Hump, was an asset to our village. Poor Fatima (still sick, still groaning) smiled a weak smile at the good tidings of his arrival, and died in her sleep that very same night.

Soon our new imam made us all forget about the old one – all except Zalanbour, that is. When he resumed his debauchery he did so at the old imam's grave. Round about midnight we would meet by his olive-shaded tombstone to raise the bottle. Arabesques of moonshine and shade crossed Zalanbour's pale face while we drank in silence. Bertollo seemed more sullen than ever. A veritable awning of a frown jutted over his eyes and I attributed this to sexual dissatisfaction. I was mistaken. It was not long before he flung himself on the grave and broke into loud sobs, his round face twisted in the grimace of a newborn infant. Zalanbour put his arm around his juddering shoulders and led him away. I stayed behind.

The olive tree rustled, shivered its branches and behold, Khadroun took shape: moonlit face, unwashed curly mane. He laid five gnarly fingers on my shoulder and told me to hurry back home, where a loud ululation had roused the villagers. He would see to the bottles.

Fatima's funeral was a quiet affair. Her children were kept at home. This time the cortège was modest. But as if to add to our number, a cloud of flies suddenly materialized. The swarming mass, indifferent to our flailing hands, covered Fatima's bier.

It was not until the shrouded body had been laid in the grave that the flies vanished out of sight. Only two or three stayed behind, snagged in the winding sheet.

I left my mother to care for Fatima's youngest daughters, while I saw to the eldest two, Fatima and Fatima.

Both were quiet, humble girls, with lowered gaze and a promise of cosy plumpness in bosom and hips. They took care of my meals, bed and clothing. I made a few half-hearted attempts to teach them to write.

They visited my bed nightly and quietly, slowly, opened their bodices. This form of gratitude betokened a simple country background, and moved me deeply.

Shaking my head, smiling, I covered up their bosoms and lifted their skirts.

One of the Fatimas lay motionless beneath me. Only a frown betrayed some inner sensation. The other Fatima clasped her hands in her young lap and waited.

I thought I might do Zalanbour a favour by taking the Fatimas along with me. He turned out to be provided for already.

By the fire I saw Batoul spreadeagled beneath him: her heaving breasts eluded his groping hands. He greeted me with a nod and a smile, without interrupting his rhythm. Batoul quickly averted her face. Their horizontal pas-de-deux was executed with a minimum display of nudity – just Batoul's breasts and fleshy thighs. Their ungainly coupling drowned out the crackle of the flames.

A shaft of jealousy pierced my heart and I flung myself with Turkish savagery onto both Fatimas. Afterwards they walked home stiff-legged, in quiet pain.

Zalanbour offered me Batoul; I declined. She covered her head and, with a quiver and roll of the hips, withdrew hastily. And all the while Bertollo was drinking and knitting his brow in disgust.

From then on Batoul avoided my scornful eyes. The sight of her squatting beside the pump rekindled my jealousy. Her pose invited immediate attack. There was not a single movement, not a single gesture she could make that did not set alight my wounded pride with voluptuous hallucinations. My tumescence cried out for release.

I went home in the hope of finding a willing Fatima to hide away with. I was disappointed: everyone was in the house, crowding around my little sister Fatima. She had found a foot among the rubble of Fatima's house, mangled, blood-soaked. Fatima held the foot in her hand and said she recognized it as belonging to her brother Abdullah – another Abdullah, the one without the flies, the martyr. 'Now he is truly dead,' she whispered.

The entire household launched into the usual hue and cry. The familiarity of the scene riled me. My hard, ungratified lust turned to rage. I grabbed the foot and swung it against Fatima's head. So much for my ill temper. Then I took the foot and went to find Zalanbour.

A sudden gust of wind blew a mass of flies, a bigger one this time, over our village. Myriads of flies swarmed around the top of my head. I warded them off with Abdullah's foot, on which they promptly settled. Try as I might, I could not drive them away. They followed me from olive tree to olive tree.

'Give it to me!' said Khadroun, extending his hand from the foliage, and I gave him the foot. The flies circled distractedly around the leafy shade until they suddenly veered away, as if on command.

When they disappeared behind the mountain, the olive tree held out a gnarly hand and returned the foot to me. Batoul, with covered head, was hurrying to the mountain. She held the edges of her headscarf in her left hand and scuttled up the dusty road in the way that was so characteristic of the village girls: swinging the legs out from the knees and barely lifting the feet from the ground. It was more of a shuffle than a trot.

I hid behind Khadroun's trunk and waited for her to come past. She let out a startled cry when I pounced on her. I would have enlisted Khadroun's help had she not surrendered so willingly. This was a disappointment. I decided that she was to have no part of me, and employed the foot. I did not want to be where Zalanbour had been before.

Afterwards she could hardly walk from the pain. I tossed the foot away. The look in her teary eyes was pitying rather than reproachful. She was prepared to give herself to me, she said.

With an affronted air I took her to Zalanbour, who made straight for her underskirted enclave.

Bertollo could bear it no longer, and before things came to a head he stomped off, kicking stones out of his path, greasy hands behind his back, drunk. I walked Batoul home in silence.

Drunk and dejected, I decided to spend the night in the mosque. The oil lamps were lit, and Imam Abou Hadba was sitting in the mihrab reading a little book. When he saw me he slipped it into his satchel.

He invited me to come and sit with him. The emanations from my mouth made him raise his hand to his nose and mumble 'Allah forgive us'. He held his two satchels in a tight grip and the last thing I saw before falling asleep was the imam settling down in another corner with his two satchels for a pillow.

I was woken by the throng of believers come for morning prayers. After I had washed I lined up with them.

During his sermon the imam voiced his concern about the village. Several villagers had died and others had gone missing within a very short time. There were djinns at large. The young girls were becoming brazen and comported themselves shamelessly in the street, responding to the young men's looks and comments in a frank manner instead of hurrying on with lowered gaze. The young men were staying away from the mosque. The young men had elected the devil for their imam – a quick look in my direction. And the village had been assailed by flies of late.

Everything (smart rap with the stick on the minbar) indicated that evil spirits had entered our homes.

The multitude listened and nodded, belching now and then in routine concentration, only moderately impressed. It was not until he said that he could not serve as imam under these conditions and that we would have to find another one to take his place that there was a commotion. Fists were waved and prayers recited. He wanted to leave the minbar, but the people rose to their feet and barred his way.

Clutching his two satchels he tried to worm his way through the crowd. When the satchels were taken from his grasp, he lost control altogether. He burst into loud sobbing, stamped his foot, foamed at the mouth and implored them to give him his satchels back.

All right then, he would stay – if we would just give him back his two satchels. Go on, please.

A few hours later, after prayers, the village elders decided to keep him under surveillance, for fear that he might abscond. Watchmen were appointed to guard him day and night, so that he would have no opportunity to flee.

Still shuddering, sniffling and hugging his satchels, he surrendered. The sheiks gave him comforting pats on the back and thanked Allah. The exhausted imam fell asleep and we all stole – shshsh! – out of the mosque on tiptoe. When I glanced back over my shoulder, I saw his thumb was in his mouth.

The sheiks were gathered together in the mosque to inspect what the village children had found. It was Abdullah's left foot, which had served as my weapon. Frowning earnestly they deliberated whether they should bury the foot now or wait until the other one was found. Since it was the left foot, they decided to search for the right one first.

The children took it upon themselves to hunt for Abdullah's right foot. We saw them running full-tilt across the village, over the hill, from olive tree to olive tree – much to Khadroun's annoyance. But their efforts went unrewarded.

At home, weeping Fatimas bathed the left foot, tenderly trickling the water with their fingers. Then they patted it dry with their long hair, which had a magpie gleam in the magic of the afternoon sun.

Khadroun, on a cloudy windswept afternoon, stood woodenly shaking his arms and fingers; his foliage shivered and a huge mass of flies, thicker than ever, swarmed overhead.

Bertollo chugged down the hill, muttering under his breath, oblivious to the unmerciful flies, faster than ever: he had just collected the rent.

Over the entire village hung a second, darkly quivering blanket of flies. All the people fled into the safety of their homes. Only the muezzin stood on top of the mosque, straining to see whether it was already time for prayer. His wife, across the street, opened the window and waved her arms, shouting: 'Oh forget the prayer and come home!'

Behind closed doors my sisters clung to my mother in wordless fright. The other Fatimas sought refuge with me, in another room. A proud manly grin played around my mouth as I gave a standing ovation to their servitude within the confines of my jellaba. The door could only be locked from the inside.

The flies took off at once when a siren shrieked into the village. Fear gave way to curiosity and all the villagers came pouring out of their houses. A police van drew up in front of the mosque in a cloud of dust, and two gendarmes with matching curly moustaches and broad shoulders alighted. One of them opened the back door to let out another passenger: a short fellow with tousled hair, stooped shoulders and a crumpled raincoat, who smiled faintly at the crowd as he went into the mosque.

After a while he re-emerged with the imam. The two village elders acting as watchmen poked their heads around the door. Two young boys climbed gingerly out of the van. When Imam Abou Hadba set eyes on them he let out a horrible cry and tried to wrench himself free. The two gendarmes restrained him.

The man in the raincoat turned to the boys and laid his hand on the shoulder of the first boy, who was presumably the less timid; the second cowered behind his companion with his finger in his mouth, trying to escape notice. In reply to the man's question they nodded and pointed to the imam.

The gendarmes handcuffed the imam, and the man in the raincoat – apparently their superior – fetched the two satchels from inside the mosque. He opened them and found two slim volumes, one containing the alphabet and the other a set of rules for young Moslems. From the size of the print you could tell they were textbooks for children.

The boys jumped for joy and, hugging their retrieved possessions, returned to the van.

As the gendarmes were leading the manacled imam away the man in the raincoat nodded to the crowd and said: 'It has taken me months to solve this case.' Then, still nodding with satisfaction at his exploit, he climbed into the van, which sirened away in a cloud of dust.

Some days after this a long procession of eleven biers wound its way to the graveyard. Ten of the biers were occupied by village elders. The imam's deception had been too great for their frail constitutions to bear.

On the final bier, which was carried by two men, lay Abdullah's left foot, wrapped in one of the Fatimas' white headscarves.

We all looked up at the sky now and then, but this time the flies stayed away.

Around midnight Bertollo and I were already tipsy, while Zalanbour was absorbed in fathoming Batoul's abundance. Bertollo drank gloomily with jutting underlip, the eyes almost completely hidden under his disgruntled brow.

I heard a rustle among the trees and got up to see what it was. Something hopped out of my path. I pelted it with stones, but they missed their mark. Too drunk to pursue the chase further, I returned to the others.

An amusing spectacle awaited me: Bertollo hunched over Zalanbour, beating him about the head with his red helmet; Zalanbour labouring on undaunted with Batoul beneath him, her eyes closed, not making a sound, just moving her head from side to side while the sweat glistened in the light of the flames. I couldn't stop laughing. Bertollo's blows rained harder and faster, and when Zalanbour roared it was not clear whether it was from pain or pleasure. He collapsed on top of Batoul and Bertollo kept up his beating.

Dripping with sweat, panting heavily, Bertollo finally concluded his castigation. He put his helmet on over his turban and left.

Batoul wriggled out from under Zalanbour's inert body, leaving him lying with his head in a pool of blood that was seeping in various directions. He seemed to have stopped breathing.

Batoul came up to me, all willingness and lubricity. I was drunk and threw my pride to the winds.

The village was imam-less once again. That morning the few surviving elders gathered under an olive tree to discuss the future of the village.

What evil has befallen our village? May Allah help us. Allah is mighty. So be it. Allah is great. What is a village without an imam? May Allah give us strength Death is stalking us. So be it. There is no escape from death. So be it. May Allah grant that we may die a death worthy of a Moslem. Inshallah. So be it.

By sundown they had reached a decision: Bertollo was to be the new imam. At that moment children came running down the hill, shouting: 'Bertollo is dead! Bertollo is dead!'

At the top of the hill we found the twisted wreck of the moped: Bertollo had crashed into an olive tree.

Crawling over the corpse was a swarm of flies which took flight when we approached. His helmet lay some distance away, gaping with shock. Bertollo's face was smeared with viscid blood, a golden tooth lay broken in his mouth, his forehead was shattered.

Djinns, the elders concluded: this is the work of djinns and flies. How could an experienced driver like Bertollo have come to grief in this way? Oh misfortune! Woe betide us! The elders launched into a raucous lament. On the crest of the hill their shadows swayed from side to side to the rhythm of their halting incantations.

When night had fallen Batoul and I went up the mountain to bury Zalanbour. But when we arrived he had vanished. Our torchlight expedition had been in vain. All we found was the dark pool of blood with flies circling overhead, as if there had been a sacrifice.

In the blistering noonday sun the bearers struggled under the burden of Bertollo's corpse. The whole village joined in the long procession following the bier, which took four bearers to shoulder.

After four days the assault of the flies had still not ended. No one ventured out of their homes. The walls of the houses, once dazzlingly white, were now covered in flies, as were the courtyards. A quivering black mass spanned the village, obliterating the mountain whence the flies had come.

Such was the state of the village when we returned from Bertollo's burial. The elders repaired to the mosque at once to confer.

After four days they were still conferring, for in the safety of our rooms we could hear them wailing from time to time. Their decision would be a radical one, that much was clear.

On the seventh day the muezzin called us to prayer. Swatting the black pest away with our hands and covering our heads with the hoods of our jellabas, we sped to the mosque.

First we prayed. Then we intoned a dirge. Then we waited quietly for the elders to announce their decision.

The eldest sheik should have acted as spokesman, but his toothless diction was unintelligible and his croaking voice inaudible. Another sheik took over, and while he made his address the first sheik banged his stick on the floor to stress the gravity of the occasion.

The speaker announced that the village would have to be evacuated and then burnt to the ground. Fire – Allah protect us against fire – was the only means of banishing this evil, which was why the village would go up in flames. At these words the eldest sheik, quaking with mounting passion, thumped so hard with his stick that it skittered out of control and he lost his balance. Lying on the floor he continued to shake and bleat until, quite suddenly, his body stiffened and then relaxed – with lowered eyelids – in well-deserved eternal peace.

We sang another dirge. Then, hoarse from our lamentations, we trooped outside and set to work.

The whole village had assembled. Possessions and children were piled onto carts. The boys walked, the older people rode donkeys. Bundles were slung over shoulders.

Rattling and braying and weeping the villagers headed to the road at the end of the village. Khadroun, planted in an earth-filled tub, swayed gently to the squeak of the wooden wheels. An old man lay resting in his shade.

A great quantity of wood was scattered about the village, over which we poured the petrol from Bertollo's moped. Solemnly, very solemnly, the wood was set alight, and we stood and watched the flames for a brief moment. Then we joined the others.

The fire spread quickly. But the flies did not go away. The village turned into a forest of flames. They danced insanely, writhed and licked. Smoke spiralled heavenwards: a gigantic black cauliflower.

The crowd started moving, singing mournful songs, without looking back. Batoul was perched in front of me on Abdullah's donkey.

Suddenly a voice cried: 'Mother! Mother! Wait for me!' We looked round and saw Abdullah's withered right foot hopping along behind, only just escaping the flames. The two Fatimas burst into jujubilation when the foot leaped onto their lap. They wept and cradled Abdullah in their arms. There was rejoicing all round.

I looked back once more and saw two shapes on the roof of the mosque, among the flames. One was tall and thin, the other – seemingly a child – was short and surrounded by flies.

Apolline

Khadroun still rustles in my memory; Bertollo's grumbling has subsided, and now that Abdullah's flies no longer cloud my vision, fresh memories show me my face reflected in the murky ditch at the end of the village.

I had slipped away from my mother, who always forbade me to idle away the siesta under the carob trees by the ditch. The bearded bachelor who lived in a little white house by that same ditch had a bad name among the villagers. My mother saw my sexual stirrings as tender quarry for his allegedly unnatural proclivities (Mother, if only you knew).

But it was he who fished me out of the water when I tripped over some unremembered obstacle and fell into the ditch. He took me into his house and bundled me into a large grimy towel. And while I waited to get dry I noticed that the walls of his dwelling were papered all over with pictures of naked women, with curved cleft forms, with fair hair and parted lips. I saw mossy deltas, dusky shadows, roseate berries of flesh. These were bound to be the munificent Sirens of the Occident, and in my heart at that very moment the seeds were sown of my love for Apolline, in whom I was to find tangible evidence of that two-dimensional voluptuousness. I loved her even before I saw her.

Apolline, my will o' the wisp, my heart's fancy. How odd that a name can acquire a taste on the tongue. This taste – I know it – is physically determined, the taste of Apolline's womanhood: the taste and pungency of oyster sauce.

At first she was Abouline in my mouth; during the halting ascent of sexual peaks (which she would not allow to be wordless) she was Appelin. But now she is Apolline, she will always be Apolline, a whisper above the widening eddies of a moist death.

I can no longer recall my first impression of Amsterdam, grafted as I am on to the vertebrae of her cobbles, the wooden wombs of her bars and weathered loins of her seedy neighbourhoods. I moved into a bedsit in Eglantine Street: a cavity in a row of decaying teeth. It was a room with all the poetry of a solitary life: dented saucepan, unmade bed, dusty window panes. Single-handed solace in the tedious gloom, love at a price on Fridays. It was not long before I met Apolline.

Taller than I, blonde, high-cheekboned, bushy-lashed, full-hipped, she was the perfect embodiment of my first, lonely golden summer in Vondel Park. She had an airy self-confidence that was unassailable. She sat at the table resting a cheek on her rosy palm, collarbones bare, smiling faintly. She shot me a glance from under her eyebrows, drew back her shoulders, jutted her round breasts, uncrossed her legs.

Soon Apolline detached herself from the framework of my shallow reverence. Her personality began to dominate my world.

For one thing, she would not have me perform my prayer duties in her presence. My devotion and loyalty to a religion were meaningless to her. She scoffed, wishing to divest me of what was to me my identity but to her merely the beads and henna tracery of folklore. She wasn't having it, she was imperious, she was all woman.

She showed me Amsterdam, a naked, omnivorous, much-loved overbearing city. She was proud to walk with me at her side: those were the days when we emigrants still had a certain exotic appeal. Each walk began with a drink in a small cafe in a nameless alley, an oasis of bicycles and bin liners and urinated writing on the wall. (The infinitely feminine gesture of feeling for her purse in her shoulder bag.)

The Amsterdam of blue jeans, tight shirts, canals:

my memory sees the city of that time in the muted shades of an eight-millimetre film. The canals dimpled and swayed with our reflections in dun-coloured water, transforming us and the city and the sky into lugubrious ghosts.

She paused by a fountain and said pensively: 'Funny how water always sounds so inviting. But you'd know all about that wouldn't you, son of the dead desert?' I wonder if the last bit was a quotation.

I can still remember the briny sweetness of my first taste of pork, the acrid shudder of my first sip of wine. I remember my first drunkenness when I broke down and wept in anonymous remorse and she consoled me in her own way: my snivelling, tearful thrusting in her luxurious confines drove her to outermost abandon.

She believed I was in need of sexual re-education. Not that I was wholly inexperienced in the world's oldest rhythm and ritual, but the way Apolline saw it I came from a country where sex served for procreation and where aphrodisiac contortions prior to penetration were not on the cards. These are her words. She could be so hurtful in her frivolous intelligence and breezy cynicism.

I often watched her reading magazines in which women complained and cooed unashamedly over debacles and delights in bed. She read them with conspicuous amusement and approval – purely, so I thought, to hurt my feelings. *My boyfriend wants us to get into all sorts of weird positions. Is it all right if I swallow it?*

Apolline made me read them all. *My boyfriend has never touched me there* (Apolline: 'Get this – their advice is:') *Tell your boyfriend this is the twentieth century we're living in; you must stand up for your rights.*

She always threatened (in jest, I hope) to send off a detailed letter if I proved unwilling to satisfy her whims (what else can I call them?) and forswear my ethnic pride and primitive principles. Adjusting to a new homeland, she said, had to start, rather literally, from the bottom. She wouldn't take no for an answer: she was so domineering, so uncontradictable, so vibrant, so womanly. So I gave myself up – reluctant, dragging my feet, with dark circles under my eyes.

I remember the first time she made me kiss her Venus shell. She lay spreadeagled beneath me, eyes misted over, hair fanning out like the seaweed tresses of a water nymph. Ali Baba was about to open the cave when she stopped me. She steered my head south-wards with considerable vigour: I resisted. In the course of an ungainly choreography a skirmish ensued, during which we became so entangled that I could no longer distinguish my limbs from hers. The beast with two backs, a multi-limbed monster. But she was unfazed by my protestations.

In the end I gave in and it was a great relief not to have to kiss dark cockscomb lips: her Botticellian complexion found a warmer, rosier match in her young core. Her face after a sticky finale was entirely flushed, radiant, and she fixed me with a look of almost mocking triumph, which made me sad because it told me how self-absorbed her world of love and sensory pleasures was.

I do not know if she ever realised how my heart ached when I left her side to rinse my mouth and returned with dead loins which she would be at pains to kindle anew.

These are moments in my dark anguished memory (as I am now, unshaven, Apolline-less, hankering) that are suffused with brightness, sunshine even, as if my memory is trying to compensate for the weak light of the bedside lamp. I have more such memories: I am a Bluebeard's castle for the daughters of my memory.

'Ah my beloved Humayd Humayd. Outside my hotel room, somewhere in the narrow streets of Fez, a muleteer is yelling so loudly that I can barely hear myself think. Here I am in your country, and it looks disappointingly like the postcards. The other day I saw an old man squatting in the shade of a palm tree. When I asked him what he was doing there he said, "Just squatting." His reply brought on what you might call a culture shock. I think I understand you better now. That is how you will undergo my love: if you're going to squat, why not under a palm tree? I have always refused to believe that there's nothing behind your inwardness. Who cares? I love you.'

A letter from Apolline. She came home kissed by the southern sun, more Apollinish than ever. God knows how many pregnant men she left behind. But she reacted to my jealousy and suspicions with a shrug of her shoulders.

I had not thought she would actually go to Morocco. The way she talked was always frivolous and each time she mentioned a trip to my 'fatherland' I thought she was joking. But she did go off one day, unannounced, and I still think it was one of her jokes.

To think of her pink and gold beauty in the dust and glare of that noisy, intractable country, of her clean elegance baking in that unmerciful climate.

Oh she had her good moments, moments of tenderness unswayed by her words. Sometimes she would lean with her hands on the windowsill and stare outside in silence, her back arched panther-like; sometimes she would raise her shoulders and fold her shoulder blades. Or she would lie naked on the bed on her stomach reading a magazine, twirling her socked feet in the air, and now and then she would glance over her shoulder at my pointless occupations, and it was at such times that I saw the ditch again and the bearded bachelor dozing in the midday heat in front of his whitewashed abode.

At other times she would lie on her back, asleep, an upturned palm beside her warm cheekbone, lips slightly parted, the nacreous sheen of the bedside lamp playing on her ribs, thighs divided by a long dark delta. At such times she was my Apolline, more than during the livelong day.

Or she would sprawl on my chest, trace my lashes with a fingernail and say: 'I can see myself in your eyes.' I could see myself in her eyes, too – foreshortened, deformed, no less puny than I always felt when I was with her.

Apolline lay in bed smoking, ghosts of blue smoke coiled in the lamplight. She drew on her cigarette and stopped halfway, coughed and said: 'It's flooding out. Could you get me a towel!'

The rumpled bedclothes exuded a soft aroma.

She laid her head on the pillow and said: 'Apolline is the name of one of the three gods who, in the Middle Ages, were said to be worshipped by the Moors. The other two were Mahound and Termagaunt. It's amusing to think my name derives from Apollo, but it doesn't, my sweet. My name comes from Apollyon, also known as the Destroyer, another name for the devil.'

She sighed and stubbed out her cigarette. It was not unusual for her to speak to me in a patronizing tone.

She turned to me smiling, ran her eyes over my body and said: 'You take your time to recover, don't you my sweet?'

What I resent is not being able to bring Apolline – she gleams like a watermark behind all my sentences, behind my existence, if you will – to life in my self-wrought language. She always eluded my grasp. Apolline was full of life, her mind latched on to each rumour in the far corners of life, she was wrapped up in it, while my own life followed a mechanical rhythm.

It is only in the photographs which I took of her and

which decorate my walls that she is whole: anywhere else and she is fragmented in my memory.

On my drunken lurchings across Amsterdam I keep thinking I see Apolline. Her words, the shake of her hair and the tap of her heels are the seams of recognition that hold the city together for me.

Distorted in the moist corners of my eyes the light of the street lamp seems to reach out for Apolline's blond hair; a peal of anonymous laughter in a smoke-filled cafe echoes Apolline's laugh in the dim grottos of my emotion. The girl behind the bar, her coppery hair catching the golden light, looks at me with living eyes (two glasses brimming with Dutch gin) and long-lashed tenderness, her baroque lips curled to expose young teeth. Tears of self-pity drip, drip, drip into my glass. Startled and repelled, she moves away.

Transparent clouds in the midnight-blue sky billow and curve like Apolline's contours under the pale sheet during her restive sleep. Red-framed sirens beckon behind deaf glass to me, wearing the same lingerie I wished Apolline would have worn had she not hated it.

Dark-bricked, grimy Amsterdam swaggers and staggers alongside my youthful mirror image in the murky ditch under the carob trees, where, reversed in watery reflection, the trees take on the shapes of tall, step-gabled canal houses jostling with the ruins of lives – plastic rubbish bags, bicycle carcasses – and where the sun cannot reach the naiads languishing under the rippled surface.

The blistering, deathly quiet of the afternoon siesta, the dusty footpaths and the olive trees, the clamour of my disorderly childhood, these provide the background to a life in Amsterdam with rare golden summers in Vondel Park, rainy Sundays, carefree boredom, lavish twilights – they constitute the difference I shared and will forever share with Apolline.

P r o d i g a l   S o n

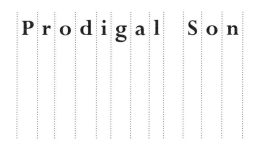

Seven years later I stood on my parents' doorstep. It was not raining.

I had not said anything to Mirianna. I had left her lying in bed. After wiping away the lingering flow of our routine convulsions she had snuggled up to me (one of those repellent habits of Dutch women), but I had got out of bed, showered, dressed and told her I was going out for a packet of cigarettes. As I closed the door behind me I caught a glimpse of her eyes, freckles and breasts, where the libidinous daze had given way to pained astonishment.

She was not to blame. It was bound to happen. Seven years had gone by since I fled the family bosom, which, as I realize now (on my way to the train that will take me to my parents), I never really understood.

What was I fleeing then and what am I returning to now? I had reached the conclusion that understanding the past was a prerequisite for accepting the present. My life in Amsterdam had never been free of doubt and unrest and I needed my parents to exorcise those two demons. I had had my fill of the heart-wrenching drunken talk of roots and loyalty to religion and destiny, of the mindless abuse of women and the fleshly, tearful reconciliations; of the sympathy (my Mirianna was so understanding, so devoted) I never asked for: I was loath to admit that my conscience was so transparent to intimate eyes.

The train lurched into motion. I did not expect to find the village much changed. In this country there are countless such villages, which, despite all the conveniences of modern life, retain a certain conservatism. My parents had settled in easily, with the blessing of their religion originating in the seventh century; Islam and conservatism share the same cradle.

'Did you go off just so you could have your way with the women of this faithless country?' my mother had said the one time I had ventured to telephone home (my father had not deigned to speak to me). 'You'll simply waste your youth on girls who can't get a boyfriend of their own kind. If you're so eager for women we'll find you a bride, a girl of your own earth and homeland and faith.' I could picture her forlorn gesticulations; my mother, a Dutch woman, had not only converted to the faith of the Arabs, but in her eagerness for assimilation she had also adopted their gestures, and even sprinkled her Dutch with Arab expressions. And she had taken a new name: Augusta had become Maimuna. My annoyance at the change was tempered somewhat by the consistency of the choice (both names mean 'Providence') but I still mourned the substitution of such a handsome model by a surrogate, which in Arabic is also a nickname for an ape. Religion evidently represents a step backwards in evolutionary terms: to convert is to ape, as my mother illustrated so patently. She believed she was better than her countrywomen waiting in Amsterdam with inviting laps for men like me. They were, as my mother put it, the 'remainders of the Creation of Our Lord'. Like all converts, my poor mother was holier-than-thou.

I still remembered the days when my father, having drunk several glasses of beer, sought to initiate me into the sexual proclivities of the opposite sex; whereby, as it happened, he did not shrink from citing my mother as an example. Once he even went so far as to refer me to the expert ministerings of an old-fashioned, fat whore. But those were the good old days. As he grew older, the beer was replaced by the Koran, and his bare words came out dressed in religious formulae which had not a whit of meaning left, but which he intoned with excessive unctuousness. All the digging for withered roots, the recourse to a terrifying God, the exhumation of a dead creed — my father had disappointed me. And although I realized that going back to my parents meant surrendering to their faith, I was different, I hasten to add, from my father in that age had nothing to do with it. I was still in my youth, I wanted to be reconciled with my youth, I wanted the freedom to choose despite the pangs of adulthood. I clung to the belief that I could turn around in the underworld of my youth and decide for myself whether the salty pillar of my wrongdoings was not worth more to me than the recompense for outright servitude. I was young and thought to give my life meaning with a mythic injection.

The train took two hours to reach my village. It was not raining.

I had never been able to banish my mother's words from my memory. In those seven years I had gone from embrace to embrace. The women were willing; it was paradise. A Turk who accompanied me on a long night of satyric foray summed it all up, complete with Turkish umlauts: 'A cünt is a cünt. What counts is the willingness of the woman.' I could almost hear the diacritic in his pronunciation of 'willingness'. True, all those women (and I am sorry to have to say this) did come from the ranks of the disillusioned and dumped, all had troubled childhoods, all were asymmetrical, although their bodily undulations went some way to make up for their mental flatness. I discovered that taste in women was culturally determined after all. Black men have a preference for broad-hipped, chubby-bottomed women with bright blond hair – preferably dyed; Arabs for soft-spoken, almost obsequious, sexually passive women, blank-eyed and pale-complexioned; Turkish men like dusty students, with dusty hair and little physical variety. My ephemeral concubines covered the gamut of plainness in all its manifestations, culminating in Mirianna (red hair, hare-lip, freckles, snub nose, sickly-sweet smell). They had busy mouths, loose legs and were besotted with foreplay. At first I had been overwhelmed by the shameful, shameless delights I owed to that trinity, but in the end I was repelled by the women's utter lack of respect during our horizontal skirmishings.

Ringing the doorbell, I swept past seven years to the furthest corner of my memory so as to open the balcony doors to the rays of a new sun and at the same time to seclude Mirianna and her sisters in darkened rooms, where I would not hear them crying.

Here I come to my own again. I rang the doorbell. Claimed by bone of my bone again. Perhaps they were praying. I rang again. And cheered by flesh of my flesh. Stepping inside I was greeted with a grunt from my father, while my mother's kiss was some time coming: she had slipped in to the bedroom to cover her head.

The smell in the house was unchanged. The furniture was arranged in exactly the same way. The carpet was still tacked down along the skirting boards to stop it flying off. The old pouf still showed no signs of having been sat on. A photograph of my younger self hung next to a cheap calligraphy. There was a bleakness about the place, as if my parents had reached the never-ending Sunday of their lives.

Slowly, discreetly, my headscarfed mother pushed the door open to peer at the unexpected visitor, and then emerged from the dusk of her room: stooping at first, eyes sunken deeply in their sockets, lips thin, teeth big, all held in place by wrinkles which, however, quickly smoothed and cleared in the full light of recognition. After embracing me and giving me her blessing she untied the thick knot in her headscarf and I noticed that her dark-blond hair was going grey. At one time, I reflected morosely, this mother had been more than worth an Oedipus complex.

Few words were spoken; everything that could be said was said by my mother's fond, slightly perturbed looks and my father's grunts. Tasting the food my mother had prepared gave me sentimental pleasure. But I was not old enough yet to be flooded by memories of childhood upon entering my old bedroom – not even of obscene manipulations and other such dreams: seven years and my mother had sluiced away all the stains. When I got into bed I smelled washing powder.

Putting my wonderland behind me was painful. The creatures of that past were reluctant to be forgotten, a smile still floated in the sleepless air, I could still hear the breathless lispings of insincere I-love-yous, the words of wisdom from bleary friends. But above all: Mirianna's Tweedledum-and-Tweedledee breasts, on which I had cried my heart out in drunken remorse. It was strange to wake without Mirianna's morning lust beside me. It was hard to go to sleep sober, without satisfying the loins. Spectres of my life in Amsterdam ogled me through the chinks in my life with my parents. There was Mirianna, who could never resist the lure of my exotic nakedness, even when its purpose was not our bed but my daily ablution. I had known her better than I had ever dared to see or admit. It was not Mirianna that I had turned against but her physical enlacement (she was so serpentine): she was still there in my head, more real than she had ever been in the real world.

My mother saw me daydreaming and knew the poison was still in my blood, and to prevent me from giving in to the urge she announced that I was to be married, whereupon a shock of nostalgia made me realize not only what I had left behind but also the absurdity of going back to your roots if you don't know where those accursed roots lie. But I did not oppose my mother's plans.

We travelled to my father's native village in northern Morocco to find a suitable bride. My mother conducted the search and soon made her pick. By tradition I was not permitted to see the bride before the wedding night. All that is required of the bridegroom is that he hold his tongue and act the perfect prospective son-in-law. I observed all these customs meekly. I must confess that I found the whole procedure arousing in a perverse sort of way. I was curious about the sexual behaviour of

Moroccan girls. I wanted to know whether Islam had influenced the mating ritual, and if so to what degree. I wanted a girl younger than me. The Moroccan air is propitious to early maturity, especially for girls: a bride of fifteen, say, would not be asking too much. At all events my bride-to-be had an impressive name: Fattúma bint Fátima bint Futayma bint Fattáma. So I went on dreaming, with bated breath.

Women and men were separated during the wedding feast. While the women's quarter was seething with last minute preparations and tumult (jujubilation and music) the men's quarter, full of bare soles and beards, was swathed in piety. We sat along the walls of the parlour listening to the imam praying in a soft voice, his eyes closed. From time to time he sighed a long-drawn-out Amen and passed his hand over his face, opened his eyes briefly while tilting his head back, then let his hands fall into his lap, which part of his anatomy, in this seated pose, formed a shapely haven for the round buttocks of boys – the very boys whom he took on his knee during Koran lessons at the mosque, no doubt with a view to inculcating some Koranic inspiration. Thus each trade merits its own time and each craft its own means – as the Arabs say. I sat among the muttering men and engaged in some muttering myself, some words from a song that came to mind, or the odd phrase I remembered from the Koran. I was dressed in a white jellaba, under which I wore a shirt of the same colour. I also wore yellow slippers and a green fez. I had been dressed in the same way for my circumcision, and the currents of air chasing through my skirt when I stood up gave me the same breezy sensation of loss I had felt then.

Suddenly the imam launched into a plaintive recitation from the Koran. Everyone joined in: the imam intoned a monotonous phrase and we echoed him, swaying our bodies to and fro.

The pious atmosphere evaporated as soon as the food arrived. The women, heavily veiled, brought the dishes up to the door and passed them to one of the men, preferably a close relative. We ate in small groups clustered around mountains of beef garnished with prunes and almonds and drowning in sauce. I sat with my father, the imam and four other extras. The imam broke the bread for us. After the *bismillahs* and the *hamdollilahs* and the *barakallahs* we started eating. The imam turned out to be an excellent raconteur. While he shared out the sauce-drenched meat with his bare hands, he regaled us with tale after tale interspersed with gales of greasy, yellowish gap-toothed laughter. Gobs of meat stuck in his beard, and now and then he paused in the middle of a sentence to lick his fingers clean – in keeping with prophetic regulations, so he reminded us. This combination of tasteful narrative with distasteful gastronomy was hilarious, but also took my appetite away. As a matter of fact everyone around me was slobbering; it was a form of gratitude and audible appreciation.

The requisite dish of couscous was followed by pastries stuffed with pigeon, pistachio and almonds, and topped with powdered sugar, an orgy of sweetness which the guests found irresistible. The young men in the company winked at me from across the room and made encouraging gestures that meant: This is the food of love, it will stand you in good stead on your wedding night. So eat, do eat. The same exhortation

was made by the imam, and also my father, in his turn, pressed the imam to go on eating; the rest of us took up the chorus, with each urging the other to eat some more. All in all the meal was not what you would call *gezellig* in the fair language of the Lowlands. This was genuine Moroccan jollity, suitably garbed in Arab reverence: this was a greasy, bearded, warm-blooded rollicking good time.

Then, finally, came what Moroccans, with typical ambiguity, refer to as 'the night of the entrance'. First the bride was taken to the marriage chamber; then, a couple of prayers and virile belches later, I followed. My mother was still with the bride, and looked at me with tear-filled eyes. The room was lit by an Aladdin lamp and the floor was strewn with piled-up rugs and sheepskins, topped with a white cloth by the way of a bed. The bride was smothered from head to foot in heavy garments veined with golden embroidery and weighed down with silver ornaments and rings. Even her hands and feet (without doubt arabesqued with henna) were wrapped, and I could not help thinking that Islam in all its mercy only prohibited the live burial of girls so that they might be buried in fabric instead. My mother embraced me and when she had given me her blessing she left, shutting the door behind her slowly so that I caught a glimpse of jostling boys' faces at floor level and a couple of inquisitive moustaches higher up.

There was a knock on the door. I opened it a little way and heard my father say that I was not to take too long. I shut the door on his words and turned to my virgin, Fattúma bint Fátima bint Futayma bint Fattáma. Her attire gave no indication of the contours of her body, and the idea of peeling off layer after layer in anticipation of what would emerge fired my imagination. To amuse myself I decided to unveil her face last of all. I set to work with due deliberation.

First I removed the heavy necklaces. Various thoughts flared through my mind. Should I kiss her or otherwise indulge in foreplay (never my forte)? The position would not pose problems, but what about the exigencies of her Venus shell? That shadowy realm of Moroccan girls was entirely foreign to me. Such biological knowledge of intimate womanhood as I possessed had been gleaned, with some demurral on my part, from the embarrassing demands made by Dutch girls, whose sexual etiquette is lacking in considerations of hygiene. In a detached, entirely non-oral sort of way (all that was fortunately behind me), I set about getting a closer look. After removing the outer garment I stroked her arms, still sleeved, but Fattúma bint Fátima bint Futayma bint Fattáma did not react, she did not move, I could not even hear her breathe.

I do not know the names of all the different garments she was wearing, but there were undoubtedly several kaftans and *gandouras* among them. Judging by the lightness of the fabrics, I would soon reach her bare skin, but I was mistaken. There was another knock. My mother put her head round the door and I shouted for her to go away. By Allah, cannot a man take his time? And I proceeded with the divestiture, faster now, but there was no end to the gaudy layers of fabric. I pulled away garment after garment, like a conjurer with a hat trick gone haywire. I thought if it took much longer my mother would lose patience and send for a stubby-fingered midwife to perform the manly deed in my stead. My efforts became frenzied. In the end I decided to tear the veil off her head in one fell swoop, and before I knew it all that remained of her clothing had dropped to the floor. In my hand I still held the veil while the rest of Fattúma bint Fátima bint Futayma bint Fattáma lay crumpled at my feet.

The Fisherman and the Sea

'See,' said the first sheik without pointing a finger, 'there goes a good, godfearing man who sets out before daybreak trusting in God, and casts his net to feed his wife and children with all that it may please God to grant him.' Nodding approval he drew deeply on his hashish pipe, which he lodged exactly in the gap between the ruins of two yellow, horsey teeth.

'Ai, by God,' the second sheik retorted, and the words came out of his toothless mouth as if a scalding morsel had burnt his tongue. 'All is in God's hands.' He, too, was smoking a pipe. His eyes reflected the calm chain-mail sea and the closing of the night with stars lingering like pearls around a negro's neck. Both men sat comfortably on straw mats, leaning against a wayward rock. Behind them the white town slept its as yet undisturbed sleep. A minaret pointed heavenward.

The fisherman they spoke of waved a *salaamaleikum* to the two sheiks. They waved a God-be-with-you in return. The rosy dawn began to stain the horizon with blood, but the fisherman had yet to make a catch. Three other fishermen, wading at a respectful distance from each other, did not appear to be having any more luck than he.

It was the fisherman's habit to cast his net no more than three times, regardless of how many fish he caught. This custom of his had often caused his wives (ever clutching a suckling to their breasts) to scoff loudly: what were the manifold offspring to eat? But the fisherman never veered from his ritual.

He was about to cast his net for the third time. Giving a groan of apprehension he started off with a prayer: 'Dear God, part the sea for me just as you parted it for Moses and his tribe. Spare me the screeching and griping of never-satisfied women and mindless offspring!'

Having said his prayer he cast his net.

'*Inshallah* — may fortune smile on him this time,' the second sheik said between two puffs.

'God gives and takes as He will,' added the first sheik.

The fisherman's prayer appeared to have been heard, for when he tried to gather in his net it would not budge.

Oh day of providence, the fisherman thought

eloquently, could Fortune be so kindly disposed as to grant me more than my old bones can lift?

But there was also the possibility that his net had got caught and he was afraid he might tear it with his joyous tugging. He took off his frayed shirt but not his much-mended, wide-legged saraballa, and dived into the waves.

'See,' said the first sheik, pointing a quavering finger, 'there goes an impious woman who, not fearing God, exposes her shame for all the world to see.'

'God help us,' the second sheik said, 'and protect her. Who knows, she might be a maiden who, having lost her reason after a night of wine and song, is now possessed by a demon and fated to wander aimlessly.'

The two sheiks were mistaken. The woman, still handsome despite her wrinkling age, was none other than the unsuspecting fisherman himself, re-emerging from the waves. As he girded up his saraballa he noticed that his chest had sprouted two dugs that were already losing their battle with gravity.

God, thought the fisherman, does not love me, for he has turned me into a woman.

But there was no time for further lamentation over his predicament as the strange apparition had already been sighted by the other three fishermen, who burst into loud jeering and began to throw stones.

'Well now, fellows!' one of them gibed, 'the sea has yielded a catch after all! This mermaid will do fine for all three of us!'

Abandoning their nets they ran towards her, thinking to teach her what they were accustomed to doing with women who led them into temptation.

The fisherman snatched up his shirt and, pressing it against his swinging teats, took to his new heels with the other foul-mouthed, raunchy fishermen in hot pursuit.

'See,' said the first sheik, 'there go three good godfearing men who will not suffer a woman to keep them from feeding their little ones.'

'These are shameless times,' nodded the second sheik, 'when a man is not permitted to labour undisturbed.'

The fisherman managed to give his tormentors the slip by ducking into side alleys en route to his house. He could hear that the three women inside were already up and busy preparing breakfast. The youngest children were elbowing one another out of bed in noisy early-morning ill temper. The women kept telling them to be quiet without, the fisherman knew, pausing in their work. Abdullah, leave your sister alone – Fatima, stop howling – you dirty dog, go and wash your face – oh go and fetch water and take that finger out of your nose.

The fisherman slunk unheard into the house through the back door. Reaching the kitchen he heard one wife tell the other: 'Woe betide our feeble fisherman husband if he returns empty-handed once more. I swear to God he will be idle tonight.'

'No, no, my sister, bedroom duties are sacred, there are no two ways about it.'

This exchange made the fisherman, his loins a burden lighter, realize that bedroom duties were a thing of the past. With a lump in his throat and lowered gaze he entered the kitchen.

Ten pairs of eyes stared at him. The women left off kneading dough, the children suspended their morning tumult, the three infants even held back a salutary burp.

The silence was broken by the eldest wife, who was also the most outspoken: 'Oh, the randy old goat! A fourth wife! He has taken a fourth wife. I knew it would happen some day! Oh, I'll pull out his hennaed beard hair by hair! The toothless devil, the flimsy-rodded lecher.'

She rose up with clawed fingers ready to scratch out the eyes of the intruder, unmindful of the child falling off her lap to the floor where it let out a juddering howl.

The fisherman was struck dumb, he could only shake his head and show the whites of his eyes. The eldest wife was restrained by the other two (whereupon two more infants slid to the floor) saying it was no fault of hers, but she was in an advanced state of hysteria and would not listen. The fisherman got away just in time and fled into the street. Behind him he could hear the fury mounting and the women hammering on the door. He had little time to come to his senses, though, for in a backstreet near the mosque he bumped into the three fishermen.

'*Alhamdolillah*,' they exclaimed in unison, 'what extraordinary good fortune!' And they lunged at him with their claws.

'What is the meaning of this?' a voice thundered behind them.

The men turned and saw the imam.

'Oh imam,' they replied, 'we found this woman on the shore. She came out of the sea like a mermaid, and as our catch was so meagre on this god-sent morning we thought God in his almighty wisdom might have sent her by way of consolation.'

A slow, white-toothed grin spread across the imam's face as he glanced round furtively, throwing dignity to the winds: 'Bring her into the mosque, quick. The door can be bolted from the inside. It is rightful for me as imam to ponder this divine miracle. Bring her inside, on the double.'

'See,' said the first sheik, 'the good fisherman's net is still in the sea. No doubt he has taken it upon himself to join the other fishermen in chastising that godless woman, as is proper for a good godfearing man.'

'No doubt,' agreed the second sheik. 'Shall we likewise do a good deed and gather in the net so that we may give him his fish, be they many or few? Perhaps the good man will reward us with a portion of his catch.'

'There,' said the first sheik, 'you have spoken wisely.'

After a while the two sheiks rose and pulled in the thrashing net. An embassy of sunlight was advancing across the sea.

'How strange,' remarked the first sheik, 'that the imam has not yet called for morning prayer.'

BENNY BARBASH

My First Sony

When ten-year-old Yotam is given a Sony tape recorder by his father, he uses it to capture the insane universe of his mad-cap, disintegrating family. What emerges is a hilarious *tour de force* – a wickedly sharp portrayal of contemporary Israeli life, which is also the story of a young boy struggling to come to terms with loss, and the weight of history.

'I found it wonderful, heartbreaking and forgiving and funny and poignant' Patricia Duncker, author of *Hallucinating Foucault*

'Their love-hate relationship has an epic ferocity which makes this portrait of a dysfunctional family both funny and heartwarming. Benny Barbash's first novel unfolds at a tremendous lick' *Daily Telegraph*

'Careers forward and back through Yotam's family history and that of modern Israel, with a breathless speed and intensity. Barbash skilfully weaves family disputes and historical confrontation into a deceptively light-hearted narrative' *Sunday Telegraph*

'Tender honesty and captivating humour' *Jewish Chronicle*

0 7472 6104 0

review

DES DILLON

Itchycooblue

Derrick and Gal are best friends. When Derrick's Da
falls sick, he and Gal set out to get him a moorhen's
egg – which they believe will cure him. The two boys
swerve through a landscape of slaggies and steel-
works, encountering the full range of life's experiences in a day that seems as elastic as childhood itself.

All that stands in their way is their fears, and mad
Mackenzie who's escaped from Borstal . . .

'The pages are stuffed full and spilling over with
imagination, they are shiny with it, brightly coloured,
and the whole book is a testimony to its transforming
power in the grimmest of realities. A child hero is diffi-
cult to do, but Dillon succeeds marvellously' *Scotsman*

'A cracking read' *Big Issue*

'Brilliantly funny' *The Times*

'A heartwarming and exhilarating read' *Sunday
Herald*

0 7472 6198 9

$\mathcal{R}$
review

RONAN BENNETT

The Catastrophist

Shortlisted for the 1998 Whitbread Novel Award.

Gillespie, an Irishman, goes to the Congo in pursuit of his beautiful Italian lover Inès. Unlike her, Gillespie has no interest in the story of the deepening independence crisis, nor in the charismatic leader, Patrice Lumumba. He has other business: this is his last chance for love.

'Bennett's writing is as lush and sensual as ripe mangos . . . The tone, which is perfectly pitched, and the exotic setting collude to evoke an era of colonial decadence' *Financial Times*

'Glowing with psychological insight . . . I have not read such a good thriller in years . . . The prose is as sharp as a whip, though subtle and poetic' Ian Thomson, *Evening Standard*

'A great achievement, an impressive testament to the appeal of strong narrative and sympathetic characterisation' *Sunday Telegraph*

'A memorable book, with a ring of deeply felt authenticity' Hugo Hamilton, *Sunday Tribune*

0 7472 6033 8

review

BEN RICHARDS

The Silver River

Nick Jordan is a young journalist who yearns for the big story.

Orlando Menoni is a cleaner from Uruguay who thinks back to the disappeared, and tries to come to terms with terrible loss.

This story of two very different men provides a moving and wholly original vision of the city in which the silver river takes on many meanings . . .

'Ben Richards's third book is all about the people who care, the people who don't yet, and the people who never will . . . Richards writes luminously about the grime and the glitter of London' *Independent*

'As suggestive and lyrical as it is pacy and slick' *Esquire*

'Refreshingly, Richards weaves his knowing sketches of London into a romantic South American tale of past revolution and lost love' *The Face*

'An intelligent, fast-paced read' *Mail on Sunday*

0 7472 5966 6

review

If you enjoyed this book here is a selection of other bestselling titles from Review

MY FIRST SONY	Benny Barbash	£6.99	☐
THE CATASTROPHIST	Ronan Bennett	£6.99	☐
WRACK	James Bradley	£6.99	☐
IT COULD HAPPEN TO YOU	Isla Dewar	£6.99	☐
ITCHYCOOBLUE	Des Dillon	£6.99	☐
MAN OR MANGO	Lucy Ellmann	£6.99	☐
THE JOURNAL OF MRS PEPYS	Sara George	£6.99	☐
THE MANY LIVES & SECRET SORROWS OF JOSÉPHINE B.	Sandra Gulland	£6.99	☐
TWO MOONS	Jennifer Johnston	£6.99	☐
NOISE	Jonathan Myerson	£6.99	☐
UNDERTOW	Emlyn Rees	£6.99	☐
THE SILVER RIVER	Ben Richards	£6.99	☐
BREAKUP	Catherine Texier	£6.99	☐

Headline books are available at your local bookshop or newsagent. Alternatively, books can be ordered direct from the publisher. Just tick the titles you want and fill in the form below. Prices and availability subject to change without notice.

Buy four books from the selection above and get free postage and packaging and delivery within 48 hours. Just send a cheque or postal order made payable to Bookpoint Ltd to the value of the total cover price of the four books. Alternatively, if you wish to buy fewer than four books the following postage and packaging applies:

UK and BFPO £4.30 for one book; £6.30 for two books; £8.30 for three books.

Overseas and Eire: £4.80 for one book; £7.10 for 2 or 3 books (surface mail).

Please enclose a cheque or postal order made payable to *Bookpoint Limited*, and send to: Headline Publishing Ltd, 39 Milton Park, Abingdon, OXON OX14 4TD, UK.
Email Address: orders@bookpoint.co.uk

If you would prefer to pay by credit card, our call team would be delighted to take your order by telephone. Our direct line is 01235 400 414 (lines open 9.00 am–6.00 pm Monday to Saturday 24 hour message answering service). Alternatively you can send a fax on 01235 400 454.

Name ....

Address ....

....

....

If you would prefer to pay by credit card, please complete:
Please debit my Visa/Access/Diner's Card/American Express (delete as applicable) card number:

Signature .... Expiry Date..............